Angel Second Class

by

Kathy Summer

Angel Second Class

by

Kathy Summer

Jarrett Press & Publications
Book Publishers Since 1994

Published January, 2001

Angel Second Class - (first edition)
Copyright © 2001 by Kathy Summer

Cover art by Thomas Massey
Editing by Nancy Alves

Library of Congress Catalog Card Number: 00-134368
Summer, Kathy,
        Angel Second Class

ISBN 1-888701-26-9

Copies of this book may be obtained from Jarrett Press, 2609 Discovery Drive, Suite 121, Raleigh, NC 27616. Phone orders and information requests should be directed to (919) 862-0551, Fax (919) 862-0991

On the World Wide Web - http://www.jarrettpress.com email - publish@jarrettpress.com

FOREWORD

Hospice employees are a rare breed. Nowhere will you find a more dedicated group. Each day they give all they have of their time, talent, resources, and most importantly, themselves. To be a hospice worker means to really be sure, with all your heart, what you believe in. One cannot look into the eyes of the dying and lend faith if there is none within.

This book is a roman a clef designed to show the type of situations a hospice nurse might encounter while working day to day. These stories are presented in order to give the reader a more comprehensive view of the very special work that hospice nurses do every day of their lives.

The story encompasses all aspects of hospice care from nurses to social workers, chaplains, physicians and nursing assistants. The ideas for the stories herein come from many different areas of nursing and life. No story is about one person. Rather they are the compilation of many different people who share a similar walk through the death and dying maze. No reference to any real person is intended or should be inferred.

DEDICATION

This book is dedicated to hospice patients and their families everywhere. And to all hospice nurses and team members. You are truly Angels Second Class. I have no doubt that you will someday be Angels First Class.

And to my family, without whose constant love and understanding I would be lost.

You are awesome!

Gentle is the care
Tender is the voice
Loving is the heart
Where angels touch the earth

ONE

Once outside the building Joan leaned her shoulders against the brick wall and perched herself on her left leg, wedging her right foot against the outside wall of the nursing home. The shadow created by the sun shining on her five foot, three inch frame reminded her how insignificant she was. Now she could take a deep breath. Trying hard not to cry, she turned her face toward the Carolina blue sky. Although she thought it was the right thing to do, she didn't like the way it had happened. So suddenly, drastically, and without a moments hesitation on either side. She had dedicated ten years of her life to this company, but tomorrow she would start looking for another place to work.

"How does one cope with the knowledge that no matter what they do or give they cannot make a situation work out right," Joan thought to herself. She didn't mind working hard, or doing the impossible, but doing the impossible day after day with no recognition of how difficult the job had actually gotten, had left her way too exhausted to deal with other important things in her life. Her children were growing up and would soon be leaving home. They had been left primarily to the care of their dad while Joan worked, and Brad, her youngest had somehow gotten the idea that he was in charge of himself. They knew her only as their mother who was always tired, always stressed, always working, and incredibly unhappy. When she looked at herself in the mirror, to say she looked everyday her thirty nine years would have been kind.

It was frightening to move on at this stage in life, but it was even more frightening to think about not moving on. With constant pressures and demands, it had become too high a price to pay. Silently, Joan bowed her head and asked God's help, "Just send me peace in my life, just help me find a good place to work." And, with a prayer and a leap of faith, Joan McRae was done with the impossibilities of a thankless job for the rest of her life.

She walked to her car, got in, and took one last look at the nursing home before she started the long drive home. Joan stopped to call her husband as soon as she knew he would be home. "Guess what I did today?" she asked her husband of twenty years.

"I don't know... what?" came the words of that familiar voice from the other end of the line.

"I quit my job." Joan had taken a deep breath and squinted her eyes as she let the words out of her mouth. She still couldn't believe what she was saying had actually happened.

James asked her, "What happened?"

"We both know it's been coming," Joan began her explanation, "Ever since the new administrator took over there has been an endless line of victims in and out of his office. Managers working hard, but never quite meeting his expectations. I sat in my office today, again, with a family member unhappy about the care we give. They know what they are seeing. They sit down and write out a four thousand dollar check every month to pay for their family member's care. They expect something in return, like the staff we told them we had working there."

"But since Cal came and brought all his budget cuts the staff won't stay because they are so tired and overworked. I can't help these people anymore was all I could think when they were sitting there talking to me. So I wrote up the complaint and took it to Cal's office. He got all mad and red faced, folded his arms in front of him like Sitting Bull and said, 'What the hell do they expect me to do knit a nurse?' I felt like saying, 'Yeah and while you're at it I need four nurse aides too.'" Joan laughed nervously.

She continued, "But who really suffers is the residents. They deserve better." A short silent pause filled the phone line between Joan and James.

"Remember Thursday night when I was late getting

10

home?" Joan asked James.

"Let me see, which night was that Joan. You're late getting home nine out of ten nights that you work. Why would that night stick out in my mind?" James replied.

"Anyway," Joan continued as if she didn't hear his last remark. Besides she knew it was true. "I was about ready to leave when I looked down the hall and saw Mike Brant standing in the hall, holding onto the hand rail with one hand, and holding his hat in the other. He had his coat on over his good clothes and he was crying. I glanced at the clock, saw how late I was, and thought about how tired I felt. Then I glanced around and knew no one would be none the wiser if I got on the elevator and left him standing there, lost in his own madness and misery. But I couldn't do that to him."

"I went to ask him what was wrong and he looked at me with the kindest saddest eyes ever and said, 'I want to go home,' I leaned in close to his ear, gave him a hug and said, 'So do I Mike, so do I, what say we go drown our sorrows in a cup of coffee?'"

"He sat at the desk while I got the coffee. As I sat down the strangest thing happened. For a short while he was as clear as you or I, it was as if he had never had Alzheimer's. He made perfect sense. He had folded his arms over his belly, stretched his legs out and crossed them at the ankles, and he was deep in thought."

"He said, 'You shouldn't be here'. I asked him what he meant and he said, 'It's almost eight o'clock and you're still here. You've been here all day. And you have children at home. You should be home with them.' He sat there awhile, deep in his own sorrowful pain... then he spoke again. 'I wish I could go back home again. When my children were small and lived at home with me and my wife, it was the happiest time in my life. I loved every day of it. Now my children are grown, one lives in Raleigh, one in Greensboro, and my boy is in the Navy. I don't know exactly where he is. My wife is sick at home with someone taking care of her, and I'm here. We're all scattered out and it will never be like it was again.'"

Another pause filled the miles of phone wire, a long one this time.

"Anyway", Joan continued, "Brad has come to the conclusion that he is in charge of himself. And our marriage and my parenting are always stressed. I had already about decided this wasn't working for me anymore when I went to Cal's office with the complaint. When I got back to the unit he called me up to his office again. He asked me to sign a statement that, as I looked it over, pinned the blame on me for the complaint, instead of his bag of magic tricks excuse for a management style, where it actually belongs."

"When I refused to sign it he threatened me, and one thing sort of led to another, and I ended up writing out my resignation and giving him just what he wanted." I said, "I'm quitting Cal, handed him the paper, and walked out."

Suddenly James was alive with alertness. "What do you mean he threatened you?"

"He threatened me with a written reprimand for insubordination if I refused to sign the paper."

"He better be careful about threatening you. There are laws and lawyers for people like Cal."

"No James," Joan quickly interjected, "I'm ready to move on."

By the time she had finished filling him in on all the details she knew things would somehow be all right. That's how things were between the two of them. No matter what she did, James was always there to catch her when she fell. "Sometimes I wish you would stop me from doing something you know I shouldn't do," she had told him from time to time. But he refused to allow her to escape responsibility of her own actions that easily. They had been married so long, and were so close, that they often knew what the other was thinking. Joan could read his inner soul, she knew what he wanted and needed, he knew what she was going to say before she opened her mouth. This marriage had survived many things but never had to endure lack of trust or love between the two involved.

Joan hung up the phone and as she walked back to her red mustang, she thought about how it was time for this marriage to have time to heal from all the damage with which the last three years of her working life had afflicted it. Too many long shifts, too many responsibilities and duties for one person to perform in a forty hour work week, that never was forty hours, had taken the girl James loved away for too long. She was anxious to put her family first in her life again. Wherever she went to work they would have a clear understanding from the beginning about what she would and would not do to earn her money. Joan pulled the car onto Interstate 85 and began the long journey home, to herself, her marriage, her faith, and her family.

TWO

Joan began her search for a new role the following day. She wasn't one to lay around licking her wounds, so she gathered newspapers and made her way to the table to search the classified ads, and drink coffee. Later, after circling a few interesting ads, she called and set up several interviews. It was a painstaking chore. One she had forgotten how much she hated. What she wanted was to go to work that day. The sooner she could put the unpleasantness behind her, she thought, the sooner she could move on to better things. She decided to apply at the local hospital.

The next day Joan dressed in her best business suit, a conservative dark blue double breasted jacket and skirt, and refurbished her resume'. She checked her nails, her stance, her hair style and when she thought she looked professional enough she took a deep breath and made her way to the car.

Once she arrived at the Human Resource office she was asked to wait for the recruiter. Her eyes searched each wall of the office. Not much was new to her. She read the required posted Equal Opportunity Employer Statement. After what seemed an eternity, the nurse recruiter appeared.

Joan had come to the hospital to apply for a job in the Emergency Room, or on one of the medical floors.

The recruiter however, asked her to consider interviewing for a job with the hospice team. "It's a young team and they need a nurse."

Joan considered the offer, with hesitation, "I guess it

wouldn't hurt to interview with the hospice manager."

Joan liked Faye Manners the first time she heard her speak. Faye had an easy going personality and spoke with an air of distinction. She laughed a lot and put Joan at ease. Joan thought she was genuine, caring, and real.

"Tell me about yourself," Faye requested.

Joan, who was silent, searched for an answer to the words. Only then did it dawn on her that she really didn't know even herself anymore. She gave the obligatory history of her nursing career, told Faye a little about her family and hobbies, and why she thought hospice could work for her.

Two days later when Joan was called with an offer from hospice, she jumped at the opportunity. She was thrilled.

A month later Joan found herself learning how to drive all over again. Not your ordinary type of driving, mind you. A whole new way of driving... hospice driving. The kind that allows you to drive ninety miles a day, do eight hours of work, and still get off work, not too late. It's the kind of driving that makes cars with twelve thousand miles on the odometer sound and ride like they have fifty thousand.

Rae taught Joan this drive while in orientation. Joan should have known what she was in for the minute Rae whisked into the office and, with her greatest smile, introduced herself and asked if Joan was ready to go. While Rae drove to the first home Joan became keenly aware that she did not possess the skills mandatory for this job, not yet anyway. As Joan learned about hospice, she was also learning something more, something that would be of great value to her in the years to come. Stop at each red light and stop sign, and briefly and thoroughly check traffic. Bring the machine at your hands up to speed quickly and watch your rearview mirror, because you don't want to get rearended when you find that driveway you're looking for in the middle of town, in the afternoon, and slam on brakes to turn into it.

"Things in the car of a hospice nurse have to be very strategically placed. It may look like a mess, but it's really a very well planned mess," Rae laughingly explained while she drove.

As Joan watched she learned that she would have to be able to hold the phone to her ear, read the directions and check the beeper at fifty five miles an hour. Not to mention sipping on coffee or eating a piece of fruit, what was commonly referred to as lunch, by nurses who preferred getting through their visits to stopping to eat.

This knowledge went into practice about four months into her job, when Joan was asked to take a student nurse from the local college with her on her route. The student was required to drive her own car and Joan cringed when she noticed the student nurse was having a hard time keeping up. When they got to the home they were to visit Joan got out of her car apologizing to the student. "I'm sorry, I forgot you haven't learned the hospice drive yet."

The student, taking it all in good humor, retorted with "Yeah... but if I spend much time with you and Rae it won't take me long."

Rae laughed out loud the Monday Joan shared with her a bumper sticker she had read in the church parking lot the day before. It read, 'Don't drive faster than your angels can fly.' The highway patrolman was not laughing however the night Joan was pulled over.

It was midnight when the family first called her to say they couldn't get their sister's pain under control. It was two a.m. when Joan got the third call and was in her car on the way to their home to see what could be done. Since traffic was light in the county Joan figured she could make this a quick trip and be back home sleeping before too long. As she neared the home she turned onto a busy four lane street and began looking for directions and road signs, trying to figure out which route would save her the most time and miles. Possibly she should have been watching the speedometer or pulled the car off the road to make these decisions.

Although she never saw the patrolman parked beside the road, Joan knew what the problem was as soon as she saw flashing blue lights in the rearview. "I was speeding wasn't I?" Joan apologetically asked the officer who walked to her car.

"Yes you were."

Joan quickly explained her actions by telling the officer that she wasn't paying attention to her speed because her attention was elsewhere.

After checking Joan's credentials as a hospice nurse, her

16

driver's license, and driving record Joan was given a warning ticket and told "You know, it's not going to do your patient any good if you get killed out here on the highway because you are speeding."

"Yes sir," Joan answered. As she pulled the Suburban, which had replaced the flashy red Mustang, back onto the highway Joan began to realize she had to be safe on the road, even if it took a little longer to get to her destination. The kindness of that police officer made her realize that the patients will wait for her a little longer if necessary, to get to them safely.

Joan also had to learn some defensive moves dealing with where she parked. One sunny day she pulled the Suburban into a church parking lot to catch up on some paper work. Her next patient wasn't expecting her for over an hour and she hated to be that early. A quick look at her watch helped her decide that she didn't have time to go back to the office. She felt that the neighborhood was safe and, besides, who would harm her in the church parking lot.

She'd been working about fifteen minutes when she saw the man approaching her car in her side view mirror. Joan checked her doors. Locked. Then, after sizing him up, she rolled down her window, just enough, so he could talk to her.

"Ma'am, we don't allow people to park here," the fifty something man told her.

Joan was quick to correct him. "Oh, I'm Joan McRae a hospice nurse in this county" she extended her hand in an effort to shake his. In other words she was Joan McRae, alias Angel.

The gentleman, looked at her for a moment then continued with his speech. "I'm the caretaker here at the church, and because of our position at this intersection we get a lot of people parking here. If you look over where you came in, it's posted with a no trespassing sign. The sign states that we will prosecute those who avoid the rules. I find beer bottles and trash here all the time. And to tell you the truth, if I let you get away with it everyone will try."

Joan could see he was not impressed with her title, and he failed to see her halo, so she put her things away, thanked the caretaker, and started her engine. "Maybe parking to chart isn't such a good idea after all," she decided.

17

THREE

Joan's thoughts were preoccupied with what makes home care and hospice so wonderful. The fact is when anyone goes into a home to provide care the family sets the tone. The families are in charge and caregivers are guests in their home. This makes home the perfect place to be no matter how sick one is. Families are super and patients tend to be very accommodating and co-operative to the caregivers who come to help them. The challenge the families have accepted would be overwhelming without some guidance. The health care team and families form strong bonds and quick friendships in hospice. They become allies in the fight against the disease. And nurses become part of their family. That was one of the first things Joan loved about hospice.

Soon Joan realized that the drive before her had passed quickly. She turned into Rebecca's driveway and shut off the engine. Joan knew by the time she had finished admitting Rebecca to the Transitions Program, which is designed for seriously ill home health patients, who in all likelihood will soon be transferred to hospice, that she did not have all the facts straight on this patient's history. Joan met Rebecca at her home just after Rebecca's arrival from near by University Medical Center. During the admission process Joan noticed Rebecca's intense pain. Joan also noticed that there were definite memory lapses, something that Rebecca's family failed to acknowledge.

Rebecca previously had several back surgeries, one of which was done to remove a malignant tumor from around her spine. She had been rushed to the hospital several weeks before with a high fever and diagnosis of sepsis, a body wide infection. These events had rendered her bed bound during her entire hospitalization. Upon further investigation Joan learned that Rebecca started having memory lapses when the fever began. When Joan asked Rebecca's husband and two daughters what their expectations from home health were, she was given goals that she feared were unrealistic.

"We were told home health would help rehabilitate Rebecca to a fully functioning state of health," they replied. This family wanted their wife and mother to be out of bed, taking care of things the way she had always done. As Joan reviewed Rebecca's medications she was immediately suspicious when she found the bottles of Dexamethasone and Dilantin, medicines to treat brain swelling and control seizures.

As Joan drove home that evening her thoughts were racing, "Surely they were all just suffering from exhaustion from all they have been through. They were all sleep deprived and tired," Joan assured herself, "Things will fall into place Monday, after they have slept." Rae briefed Joan Monday morning, in post weekend report, about her visits to the home Saturday and Sunday. She had given Rebecca's medication twice a day through her port-a-cath, a plastic reservoir located just under Rebecca's chest, leading into a large vein, without problems.

When Joan walked into Rebecca's room for her visit that afternoon she had no idea that she was about to begin one of her most memorable nursing experiences in twenty years. Rebecca was sitting up in bed eating, "Well, how are you today?" Joan asked her.

And in the cheeriest voice, as if she had not a care in the world, Rebecca replied, "I'm just fine and how are you?"

Rebecca's daughter, Kim, had taken time off work to care for her mother that day. Her husband, Bill, was there as was her youngest daughter, Sheri. Joan began teaching them how to protect Rebecca's skin from breakdown and about diet needs for increasing her stamina. They asked lots of questions about her medications. There had been many changes during the recent weeks in the hospital and the family was concerned about why she was on all the new medications.

Suddenly, that pharmacology class Joan struggled through

years ago was making sense to her. She had reviewed Rebecca's medications over the weekend and knew from the medicines she was on that the doctors were trying to use different drugs together to increase the pain relieving effects of the drugs she was on. "Sometimes no matter how much morphine you give, it won't stop pain by itself. Sometimes doctors order Ibuprofen and other additional medications to give better pain control," Joan explained to the family.

To help them temporarily, until Joan could get patient information sheets on all Rebecca's medicines, she wrote out what each medication was given for, when to give it and how to give it.

"How do you feel about learning how to give her antibiotics through a line I leave in her port? You won't have to stick her with needles or anything. I'll do all that part for you," Joan asked Kim and Sheri.

After some discussion and questions Kim and Sheri both said they could do it, and Joan felt very comfortable with their ability to be taught.

Joan assured them, "I will not expect you to do anything you are uncomfortable with, and I will be there for each antibiotic administration until you are sure you can do it alone," Joan told them. "And there is a call nurse on twenty four hours a day if you have any problems."

They worked on their technique and Joan wrote out each step of the procedure. She watched as Kim gave the medication. Sheri read each step while Kim performed the task with amazing precision. Joan watched admiringly as the two worked so lovingly to learn how to care for their mother. She almost laughed out loud when Kim reminded Sheri, "It's my turn, you did it last time."

Rebecca's family cared for her every need. She was attended twenty four hours a day and her family members worked well together. She was their priority. Kim, Sheri, and Bill took care of Rebecca while Rebecca's three sons took care of Kim, Sheri and Bill. Other friends and family members shopped and ran errands, and their minister visited often for emotional and spiritual support. In Joan's eyes they were exactly what a family was suppose to be, coming together to help each other in a time of crisis.

Over the next few weeks Joan saw a change in Rebecca. "How are you today?" Joan would ask her.

With each visit her voice was cheerful and she would say, "I'm just fine." But with each visit Joan noticed the lines of Rebecca's face deepen. Her smiled waned, and her look was weary. Rebecca would turn away while Joan talked to her and say "oh," under her breath, as she struggled to reposition herself in the bed. Joan contacted Rebecca's doctor four times to increase her pain medication.

The air was warm with a nice breeze blowing when Joan arrived at the home on a Friday morning in late April. Joan closed her eyes and took in several deep slow breaths. Breathing in the early spring air made her forget, for a brief time, the seriousness of the disease with which the patient she had come to see was battling. The euphoria of the spring weather stopped however, the minute Joan walked into the bedroom and saw Rebecca. "Oh my God," she whispered to herself. After she gathered her emotions she asked Bill, "How long has she been like this?"

"She's been getting steadily worse all night," Bill's voice almost cracked with exhaustion and emotion at the relief of the nurse's arrival.

Rebecca was not talking, she appeared to be sleeping but her teeth were clenched tight, as were her hands. Tight fists, clenched. Her body was very still, and she was not eating, drinking, or taking any of her medication. Her face was without color. "She's too pale," Joan said, the thought stuck in her mind, paralyzing her temporarily. She had to force herself to re-focus.

At this point, Joan knew it was time to talk seriously to this family. She asked them, "Tell me what your understanding of Rebecca's current condition is."

They hesitated, lost in the meaning of her words. She tried again. "Have the doctors said anything to you about spinal or brain cancer. Have any of the doctors talked to you about hospice for Rebecca?" Joan watched as the looks on their faces changed almost instantaneously from faint hope to despair. It hurt her to have this conversation with them, but as hard as it was for her, she knew it was much harder for them.

"He said something about hospice but I didn't know what

that was," Bill eventually responded.

Joan excused herself and went into another room to call the primary physician and asked him what he had told this family. She asked the nurse to ask him, "What is the extent of Rebecca's disease, is it possible that Rebecca has spinal cancer, and if it has spread to her brain?" While Joan awaited his return call, she talked to the family more. They wanted to know what hospice was. They didn't understand it, and how it applied to Rebecca.

The phone rang, jolting all of them out of their shock. It was Rebecca's primary physician.

He talked to Joan and told her, "Yes, I've told this family that they needed hospice, and that Rebecca definitely has cancer in her spine, brain and most likely everywhere."

Joan felt solemn when she hung up the phone. This was not going to be pleasant. "What am I doing in this situation?" Joan whispered to herself. She shook at the thought of what she was about to do. Her face grew flush and hot and she wanted to cry. She wanted to run away, to do anything rather than face Rebecca's family, do what was next, walk into the next room and speak. She thought she was going to vomit. She told them she would be back shortly and went outside to get some fresh air.

After pulling herself together Joan gathered the family and told them what she had learned from the doctor.

"Are you telling me my mama's not going to get better?" The words so innocently came from Kim's mouth.

And although they were some of the hardest words she'd ever spoken Joan knew she had to be honest, "Yes, that's what I'm telling you," she softly but firmly replied.

Joan could see the horrible impact of reality spread through Kim's body like a raging river. It first swelled in her chest, then rose up to her throat and finally flooded out her eyes. Sheri was more composed. Joan knew she had figured out the truth ahead of the others. Sheri turned to console Kim. Bill turned away from them all and looked out the window, tapping the knuckles of his right hand on the window sill, not speaking at all, only staring.

Joan solemnly finished her work with Rebecca and comforted the family as well as the moment would allow.

Once back in the office Joan called one of Rebecca's doctors and asked for an order for intravenous or subcutaneous morphine, continuous drip. After much consideration, the physician decided that subcutaneous morphine was the best bet. They needed to continue her antibiotics through her port for pain control and were already having trouble keeping Rebecca from pulling that needle out. Joan had replaced it several times now. Bill felt sure that if Joan put an IV in Rebecca she would only remove it.

Joan paged and talked with Laura, the social worker for the hospice team. "You better call this family, I just dropped a bomb on them and they are in shock, I know they have lots of questions." Laura assured Joan she would call right away and meet with them as soon as possible. Joan filled out all paperwork to transfer Rebecca to hospice.

It was after five when Joan returned to Rebecca's home with the morphine pump which had been prepared to deliver the specified doses Dr. Pike had ordered. The family was all present and Joan warned them that she did not know what would happen when she started the morphine. "She may relax and come back around, or her breathing may slow and if it does I'll call Dr. Pike and see what we need to do," she explained. Joan began the subcutaneous drip slowly, with a low dose of morphine. She taught the family how to give extra medicine by pushing a button on the strange machine she would be leaving on the bed beside Rebecca. Joan watched for some response from Rebecca. By eight thirty she had the drip up to seven milligrams per hour and did not feel comfortable going any higher that night. It was getting late and she had to confer with the doctor… and she had other patients to see.

After consulting with Dr. Pike, it was decided that the morphine would remain at seven milligrams per hour and Joan would re-check Rebecca the next morning. Rebecca's respiratory rate was unchanged from when they had started the infusion. Joan said good night to the exhausted family and left.

It was ten thirty by the time Joan got to Rebecca's home that Saturday morning. Rebecca was still sleeping but her hands were relaxed and her teeth were no longer clenched. Joan told the family that this was good in that it showed some sign of pain control. She instructed them on getting fluid in Rebecca if she awakened. She called them on Sunday, there was nothing new to report.

By Monday there wasn't much change. Rebecca was still not taking in any food or water. Joan felt sure that it was time to call the family in. Rebecca had been without any nutrition for four days now. Her pulse rate was up to one hundred and twenty, from eighty beats per minute, because she was becoming dehydrated. And her blood pressure was dropping, all signs that Rebecca was entering the actively dying stage of life. Joan explained the dying process to the family and told them, "What you need to do now is look at Rebecca, take care of her needs at this time. If she's hurting, give her pain medicine bolus. If she's hot cool her off with cool water baths. Talk to her and make her as comfortable as you can, and if you run into problems that you can't handle, my phone needs to ring."

The family set about making all arrangements for Rebecca's funeral and her friends came. Kim and Sheri bought her a beautiful deep blue dress, to match her eyes. They chose jewelry for her from her box, and went to the florist to pick out her casket spray. Bill and his sons chose the casket and headstone.

On Wednesday afternoon, after six days with no nutrition Bill walked by Rebecca's bed. "May I please have some water?" the words he thought he heard froze Bill in his tracks. He quickly looked to the bed where his beautiful wife laid. She was smiling at him, awake as if she had just awoken from a good night's rest. Bill eventually was able to respond to her wish. Joan got a 911 page to go to the house as soon as possible.

"Sure... I'm on my way," she responded to Faye who had paged her.

It was almost too much for Kim to bear. She had set herself for the big chill and this sudden thaw caught her off guard. She was crying and inconsolable when Joan arrived. Rebecca wanted to know what had been going on. As soon as Joan found out what happened she was in touch with Laura again, "You have to go back down there today and take a bereavement counselor with you, they are in worse shape now than they were last week."

Joan could not believe what was going on, as she walked out of the house to her car she turned her eyes to heaven and asked, "Are you trying to teach me a lesson? I know you are still in charge down here but she had all the signs of coming your way, you shouldn't have sent all the signs if you weren't going to open the gates," Joan shook her head and shrugged her shoulders. Then she thought of a Bible verse she had read about not even the angels in heaven knowing the date or the time, so what made her think she could know. Next time she would tell people that it wouldn't be over until it was over, then she wouldn't have to call out the damage repair team.

Laura and Mike, a bereavement counselor, had visited Rebecca's home a few hours after Joan left. They had not only talked to Kim and the others, they talked to Rebecca and told her how seriously ill she was. And why all these people were in her house. It wasn't easy to assess how much of the conversation she comprehended, because the cancer had gotten worse as each day passed, but Rebecca did not seem surprised by the news. Never again did Rebecca ask questions or talk about any of these events. She never mentioned her cancer again and, after that day, any time any one went to see her, all she ever said when asked how she was today was, in her cheeriest voice, "I'm just fine and how are you?"

The family began to fall into a routine. Someone was always with Rebecca but they went about their work and routines and relieved each other. For seven weeks they watched the slow changes. Some days they could get food and medicine in Rebecca and some days they couldn't. Rebecca continued to take days of "rest." The pain continued to worsen and Joan and Dr. Pike stayed in close contact. Rebecca's morphine had to be increased almost weekly. Joan was amazed at the level of morphine Rebecca was able to take and still carry on conversations. Just how much the human body could endure never ceased to amaze Joan.

Kim and Sheri had both talked to Joan at different times about what they were going to do "after this was over."

Kim talked to Joan one day when the two were alone with Rebecca, who was having one of her sleep days. "I would have never thought that this could happen to my mother," Kim said, "I don't know how I'm going to get through this." Joan simply let her talk about her feelings. She began to see the family members were moving toward a new phase. As Rebecca was dying, her whole family was going through the grief process. Joan could see that they were ready for this to be over. They had had time for it to sink in. They had taken good care of their loved one at a critical time, and they were physically and emotionally tired from all they had suffered. They were tired of watching Rebecca die a little at a time.

Kim and Sheri had each asked Joan questions about their chances of getting cancer now that this had happened. Joan had advised them to talk openly with their doctors and had given them some information from the National Cancer Institute and advised them to write for more information. The two had asked Joan for recommendations of a doctor who was up on the latest in cancer research. Joan had talked to them about diet and exercise and their link to cancer. She had tried to help them not to be alarmist. She shared with them a lesson she was learning too. "Live each day for what it is. Be happy for today and try not to waste today worrying about tomorrow."

Bill stayed busy all the time, working outside on the farm when the children were with their mother and cleaning inside the home when he was there alone.

Kim had wondered, "How can he keep going on such little sleep."

He kept telling her he was "all right."

Joan told the children that, "Bill was handling the anticipated loss in his own way, the only way he could, by staying busy. He will sleep later, when his wife is gone, and that will be good for him."

Bill began to follow Joan out of the house after her visits. He would ask the questions he couldn't ask in front of the others. He had shared details of his marriage with Rebecca that Joan was sure the children did not know.

"This has been going on a lot longer for me than it has for them," Bill began, "Looking back, Rebecca has known for a long time that this cancer would take her life. She used to take such precautions to protect herself from any little germ. After they diagnosed her ovarian cancer in 1984 and treated her, she became afraid. Every little pain would send her to the doctor to have an x-ray or test. And she would agonize over it until the results came back. She never had any true peace after the first cancer started."

One sunny afternoon Bill asked Joan what would happen to Rebecca in the end. "So how does this death thing actually come about, and how will she get through it?"

Joan sat on the red brick steps to carefully consider her answer to his question. She was overtly aware of the presence of potted tulips, yellow, in the spring sunlight. Flowers that Rebecca had planted and Bill had tended with such gentle care. "I am not sure if her cancer will just continue to grow until a vital organ or vessel is overtaken or if she will die of heart failure."

"Why heart failure?" Bill asked in surprise.

Joan explained, "Because Rebecca's heart has been beating rapidly for so long and has began having irregular beats, it may be getting tired." She told him that the heart can usually take working extra hard only for so long, but that it was different with each person. "And, because Rebecca is young, it may take longer for her to go through this."

Joan could see that she still hadn't completely answered his question, after she thought for a moment she continued. "As for how Rebecca will get through it, she will have help. Some of us believe that angels will come. When she starts talking about seeing people who are dead or seeing the Lord, her time is probably close," Joan chose her words carefully. "She will close her eyes and awaken to a bright light or a beautiful garden and she won't be afraid or alone. Death is but for a brief period and then Rebecca will no longer hurt." Joan told Bill what she thought he could understand, and what he needed to hear. She knew this family was active in their church and close to God.

"Okay, well,... I'm ready when He is. I don't want her to suffer anymore." Bill was dry eyed but Joan made her exit as fast as she could. She cried all the way to her next visit, something she had never done before. Perhaps she was tired or stressed, or maybe she had gotten unexpectantly close to this situation.

She remembered the day Sheri asked her, "How do you work with hospice all the time?"

Joan had told Sheri that she had to remain objective, that to be strong for the family she had to professionally distance herself and could not afford to be overly emeshed. Famous last words, she thought. "Liar," she said looking at her eyes in the rear view mirror.

The call wasn't a total surprise. Joan was on weekend call. On Monday morning she was getting ready for work when she was paged.

Kim was on the line, "Joan, I think she's dead," her voice was strangely calm. "I don't see her breathing and I can't get her to talk to me and her skin is very white."

"I'm on my way," Joan told Kim as she hung up the phone, grabbed her car keys and hurried out to her car. She arrived at the home twenty minutes later.

Joan knew the minute she walked into the room that Rebecca was dead. She went through the legalities she had to in order to be sure that Rebecca had no pulse, respiration, or blood pressure. She asked a family member to get Bill from work.

While she waited she bathed Rebecca. Her eyes fell on a picture of Rebecca on the table beside the bed. Rebecca had a ribbon in her hair. Joan opened a dresser drawer and found a red ribbon. She placed it in Rebecca's hair as best she could. Then she applied what Kim had told her was Rebecca's favorite cologne. Joan knew that this family would remember this moment for the rest of their lives and when Bill kissed his wife for the last time Joan wanted her to smell the way she used to, before her body was consumed by cancer, and she didn't want the kiss to leave a salty taste on his lips.

When Bill entered the room Kim and Sheri broke down. He took off his hat, went to the bedside, kneeled down and gingerly touched Rebecca's hand. He leaned and kissed her cheek. His nose fell directly where Joan had placed the cologne.

Their minister came in just behind Bill. He gathered the family together and had the sweetest prayer Joan thought she had ever heard. After it was over, Joan looked around to see what else she needed to do. Her eyes were pulled to Rebecca's left hand laying on top of her chest. Joan removed the small diamond ring from Rebecca's left hand and handed it to Bill. He gently examined it as if for the first time, and the last time, and placed it in his pocket.

FOUR

Joan sat in the hospice nurses room in the office where on a Friday afternoon she witnessed an attitude she had almost forgotten could exist in nursing. The nurses were giggling and joking as they finished their work for the week.

Faye came into the room and told the nurses, her nurses, "You guys had better get to work, you're making too much noise, there is work to be done, after all."

Chris started it, with a devilish smile and a gleam of mischief in her eye, she shot Beverly a knowing look and winked.

Beverly nodded and the singing began. "Mean and ugly mother, mean and ugly mother, I would have no other than my mean and ugly mother," the song was followed by intense laughing from all the nurses.

Faye threw her hands up in the "I give up" way and shook her head, but Joan could see her laughing just as hard as all the others.

Faye was an excellent leader. She taught Joan that you do better if you lead not as much by the book as by the heart. She never criticized her staff, openly or in private. She seemed to see only their good traits and concentrated on the positive things they had to offer hospice and each other. She had high expectations of her staff. They were case managers and were expected to fulfill that role. Her role was to give them the support they needed to do their jobs. Joan knew she would learn more from Faye than she had ever learned in a work situation in her life.

Rae came into the office. She came through the door laughing and hugging people, "How are you?" she would say, as she hugged each one.

"How does she do that?", Joan wondered.

Shortly after that Becky, a hospice nursing assistant, came in. "Joan would you come and take a walk with me?" she asked.

Joan sensed a seriousness about Becky's request so she decided to let the paper work go for a while and followed Becky outside.

Becky finally spoke. "Look I like you, we all do, but you have got to loosen up a little. The patients don't know how to take you. They say 'who is that girl you sent down here, she sure is professional?' They don't know how to take the new nurse who doesn't smile a lot and writes a lot of notes. I tell them you came from a place where you were under a lot of pressure and had to be serious. But in the home such behavior seems well... cold."

"And, although I know you're a good nurse, these patients care a lot less about your credentials than your personality. To them you're not just their nurse, you become part of their family. Comic relief is an essential ingredient in the make up of a hospice nurse, and if you don't learn to relax you're never going to last here."

When Becky finished Joan felt strangely bonded to her. "I wasn't aware that it showed, I see Rae and the others but that doesn't come natural to me. I thank you for being so candid, your point is well taken. You showed a lot of courage and caring, I know this wasn't easy for you to say," Joan responded.

From that day on Joan smiled every time she saw Becky. At first it was a forced smile but as time passed it became more natural. Then it got almost silly. They walked by each other and made faces in the hall, then broke into laughter, like two little girls.

Joan also learned how to smile her best smile with others too. Not only at work but at home. Her patients responded to her warmly once they knew she was genuinely concerned for them. Her family grew in happiness more and more each month. By the end of her first year with hospice Joan's old friends from the nursing home didn't recognize her.

After a short weekend get away to the beach Cheryl had

commented, back at the nursing home where she and Joan had worked together, that she had, "Spent the weekend with someone who looked like Joan McRae but she sure didn't act like her."

Her family was reaping the benefits of Joan's new joy. She was in the kitchen cooking dinner one day when James came home. "Quick boys get the camera!" He said.

"Why do you need the camera?" Joan asked him, as the two teenagers came into the room to see what was going on.

"I want to take a picture of what a wife in the kitchen looks like." The three men in her life roared with laughter. And Joan laughed at them laughing at her. She was finding time now to do the things she had wanted to do but was always too busy. It was a great feeling to finally have time to get to her goals outside of work. It was wonderful to see her family so happy.

"Oh, by the way I'm an angel," Joan told James one afternoon, as he was putting his things away after arriving home from work.

He stopped emptying his pockets in the valet, and responded "An angel, who says?"

"Oh, my patient's family... said I was an angel... straight from heaven mind you! So don't mess with me," she laughed and teased him as she kissed his cheek.

"Yeah, well those people don't know you like I do, they don't know you're really the devil." She caught his smile from the corner of her eye. Joan left the den, laughing, to change her clothes.

She thought about her day. When she had left her last job she had taken the first offer she had been given. She and James had talked about how if it didn't work out she would stay only long enough to find something she really wanted to do. She had, after all, been a manager before and now she was only a staff nurse. Joan was surprised however at just how much she was enjoying her new role. It had been a long while since she had felt so appreciated in the work place.

She reached into her pocket and took out a card. It had arrived at the office from the family of a patient Joan had cared for recently. The hand writing read 'thank you for being my Dad's angel'. Joan kissed the card and placed it in her dresser drawer, along with the other cards, her own collection of tokens of appreciation from her patients and their families. "It was my pleasure" she said, as if his son could hear her.

When she went for her evening exercise she said her evening prayer and asked for guidance in her work. She asked God to send her wisdom, compassion, and energy to do her work. She asked Him for guidance in her marriage and family life too. She thought about her friends she had left behind, bonds that had been broken, and gave thanks for new friendships forming, new bonds.

Over that first year Joan's prayers had changed. She prayed for her safety but the majority of her prayers were for others. Perhaps for the first time in her life Joan could see a bigger picture than herself. She was becoming part of something that humbled her, yet was driving her on to a greatness she had never experienced. She asked God to send her opportunities to help others every day. It would be her gift to Him. And opportunities to help she got!

I'm going to a place where you cannot yet come
I don't know what I will see there or who I'll meet
But I'll tell them all about you and your love
I'll prepare a place for you and
When it is your time I'll join your angels
We'll come to you and lead you home
But for now I'll kiss you and say good-bye to
The greatest love I've ever known
Because I'm going to a place where you cannot yet come

FIVE

Annie sat by Henry's bed on a high stool she had gotten from the kitchen. Her thin pale fingers stroked his white hair ever so gently. He did not respond to her touch now. He was close to death. His breathing was labored at times but Annie knew what to do. Chris and Joan had taught her well and she remembered all that they had told her.

Joan sat in the recliner beside Henry's bed, opposite Annie. She could look at this picture all day and never get tired. Annie was tall and slender. Her hair, now thin from age, was pulled up on her head, and she had strong deep brown eyes. Annie had worked hard all her life. She had happily worked along side of Henry in their family business for thirty years.

"Annie, can I get something for you?" Joan asked her.

"Yes please," Annie smiled and nodded toward the kitchen, "coffee."

Joan got Annie a cup of coffee. "Where are the children?"

"Oh they left for a little while, to go to lunch." Annie replied and began sipping her coffee.

Joan loved Annie's stories about her life and telling them seemed to be therapy for Annie. Today Joan asked Annie, "What was your life with Henry like when you two were first married?"

Annie's eyes brightened instantly as she remembered. Her voice was weak from exhaustion. "Well, I remember one time I was outside washing clothes with a wash board, and I saw a little black truck with spoke wheels coming up our drive. I think it was one of those early model T's or maybe a model A, I don't know. But a traveling salesman got out of it and came over to me trying to sell washing machines."

I told him, "You see that man down there in that garden? Well that man needs a tractor to work those rock hard fields a lot more than I will ever need a washing machine, now you get on out of here."

"He wouldn't take no for an answer. He said, 'If you don't mind ma'am I'm going to walk down there and talk to him for a moment.' I said O.K., but we don't have five dollars for a washer, so don't you go trying to sell him one."

"About a week later here came that same little black truck, up the drive again, with a new washer on it. Henry called it an anniversary present, and I cried for a week because he didn't have a tractor, couldn't use the blame thing for a month." Annie leaned over to kiss Henry's head while Joan went to wash her hands before caring for Henry, she quickly wiped her eyes so Annie wouldn't see.

Joan measured Henry's vital signs. "His heart beat is faster today, around 110 beats per minute, and his blood pressure has dropped some to 90 over 50." Joan explained the significance of these changes to Annie. "As he becomes more dehydrated this trend will continue, his heart will beat faster as it tries to circulate less blood volume to the body, and his blood pressure will keep falling as he becomes more dehydrated. You are doing a good job keeping his temperature down by bathing him. How are you doing giving him the medications?"

"I think we're doing fine," Annie replied without hesitation. "I am giving him the morphine every two hours before we turn him, it keeps him from having breathing problems when we do turn him. And we give him the Lorazepam when he needs it." Annie had kept a good record of all that she was doing. She was trying hard to do all she could for her Henry and Joan admired her for all she was doing. Annie spoke with some concern, "I'm surprised he's still here."

"He doesn't want to leave you. You have had a wonderful life together, you've built a good home and raised a great family. That's not easy to give up," Joan told her. The words seemed to ease Annie a little. "Have you been able to sleep Annie?" Joan knew the answer to that question before she asked it.

"Well you know, not too much, I'll sleep later. I take naps in that recliner beside the bed between turning him." Then Annie broke the serious mood with a wry smile. "Oh!" she exclaimed as though she had just remembered an important vital statistic that the nurse before her just had to know immediately. "I want to thank you for sending Mike over here yesterday, he came at just the right time, you know that preacher that was here?" Joan nodded. "Well," Annie continued, "He stayed and stayed, he's new you know and I don't think they let him do much, I guess he was bored, but I can only talk to someone I don't know for so long and I needed him to go. I kept giving him hints but he didn't take them. Finally, Mike came in and then I told the preacher I needed to talk to Mike privately. After he left I told Mike to come back today and I collapsed in that chair for a couple hours." Joan and Annie laughed like two old friends.

Annie asked Joan, "Is Henry going to hurt when death does come, will he struggle?"

Joan told Annie, "The medication is keeping Henry from fighting for air. I don't think he will hurt. But he can still hear, so feel free to talk to him clear through to the end."

Annie found Henry's favorite music and they put the tape in a player and laid it close by his pillow so he could enjoy the sounds he loved. Joan asked if Henry had worn cologne and Annie retrieved a bottle of Old Spice from the bathroom. Joan placed the cologne on his hair, chest and face. She wanted Annie to have the fondest memories possible from these last days with her beau. When Annie kissed him for the last time she wanted him to smell like the man she loved, and the man she loved smelled like Old Spice.

"Annie, I know this is hard for you now, it is very much a labor of love. But I hope in time when the dust settles and you have rested, you will be able to look back on all of this and find comfort in the fact that you were here for Henry when he needed you the most. You should be very proud of yourself, this is no easy task," Joan spoke the words with so much tenderness she almost didn't recognize herself.

Joan and James had been married for twenty two years and working with Annie allowed Joan to help someone she admired if, for no other reason, the fact that this had been a long, strong marriage, something Joan valued. "How long have you been married?" She asked, Annie.

"Forty nine years, it would be fifty years this April. I wanted to make that one, I was so hoping he would make it 'till then, but it's okay, he tried his best," Annie said smiling, tenderly stroking Henry's hair again.

Annie saw Joan to the door and waved good-bye to her. The next day Joan was so busy that she had asked Laura to look in on Henry for her. She got the news when she finally got back to the office that afternoon.

"Henry died at eleven this morning. He died in Annie's arms."

Laura told Joan that he had gotten into some breathing difficulty a few minutes before he died, and Annie had held him and told him, "You've got to go on home now, I'll see you again, but you're too sick now to stay here with me." Henry looked at Annie one last time and she kissed his cheek. She closed her eyes and took a deep breath, breathing in his spirit, his essence, his Old Spice, when she opened her eyes he was gone.

SIX

Spring was heavy in the air, as evidenced by the daffodils blooming in the garden outside The Family Care Center. Looking at them reminded Joan McRae that life was eternally beginning again. She walked past the home's pet dog as she neared the door. Joan stooped to pet the brown and white heinz fifty seven as she passed. "You're a sorry sight for a dog," she told him, "But at least you're well behaved and it's easy to feel sorry for you." Joan petted the dog for a few minutes before she went inside of the home. He enjoyed it and began to look forward to Joan's visits.

The retirement home was beautiful. It was in the country and surrounded by beautiful shade trees. It had a front porch with eight rockers. One for each of the six residents who lived there, and two for the caregivers. In the summer Rose would get hulls filled with baby lima beans and snap peas. The ladies would sit on the front porch and shell beans and talk about their lives. They liked to talk about their home with Joan during her visits.

One day she sat out on the porch with them, grabbing a handful of beans to shell she asked each of them, "What do you miss most about being young?"

Maylena had responded, "I wish I could get in my car and drive down the highway just one more time. I really miss my car." All the other ladies agreed they missed driving. Joan said, "You know what Maylena, if you could see the roads now you might change your mind. There are so many more people now than just a few years ago and the traffic is terrible. They can't

38

build roads fast enough to keep up and it's so crowded. It's not fun driving now. I remember when I was little we would go out for a drive on Sunday, people don't do that much anymore."

Joan loved this visit. She started looking for Martha as soon as she entered the double glass doors, this day, and passed by the beautifully decorated foyer. "Good morning everybody," she said to the four residents who were sitting in the den. Martha was not among them this day.

As she neared Martha's room she heard the two voices discussing what would be worn to the doctor's office the next day. Joan knocked on Martha's bedroom door and entered.

Rose, the owner of the home, was standing by the closet removing outfit after outfit and waiting for Martha to disapprove every one, for various reasons. "What about this one Martha?" Rose would ask as she held a garment up in front of her.

Martha, a Jessica Tandy look alike, only shook her head, made a tsk tsk sound with her mouth and cited yet another reason that the outfit wouldn't work, "Too big, too small, I don't like that color," or, "I never wore that one when I wasn't sick."

Rose threw her head back with each rejection in a mimic of exasperation. "Now Martha you know I do have to go cook in about two hours so let's finish this before then, OK?"

"You see how she treats me?" Martha turned to Joan for camaraderie.

Joan, who had sat on Martha's bed, laid back and laughed out loud at the sight of it all. "Martha the truth is that I do see how she treats you, like a baby, everyone should be so lucky to be pampered the way you are." Joan leaned over and kissed Martha on the forehead. "How are you today?" she asked.

Rose pulled up a chair and she and Martha filled Joan in on how things were going. Martha had been placed in Rose's care because her doctor had determined that she was no longer able to properly care for herself at home. Martha's only two surviving family members lived too far away to be with her and were thrilled, and lucky, to have found an opening at Rose's just when they needed it.

Martha had improved since coming here. Her appetite was better and she was getting her medication on the correct schedule. Rose reviewed her record with Joan and they called

Dr. West for refill orders on the medications that were low. Joan also reported that Martha was weak and wasn't drinking enough fluid. But, overall, she was much improved over the state in which her family had found her that first day. Martha had been found all alone in her home, where she had fallen, and was confused.

Joan encouraged Martha to keep eating and to try to drink more fluids. She asked Martha how she liked her new home. Martha looked around the room she was in. Rose had lovingly wallpapered each of the bedrooms with beautiful early 1900's style wall paper and bought furniture from the same time period. The resident's beds were piled high with as many pillows and quilts as they desired. And the home had an exercise room where Rose led them in exercise in the late afternoon. Each resident had their own place at the table. Everything in the home was designed with these elders in mind.

"I love my new home" Martha told Joan. "I think I'm very lucky. Do you like coming here?" she asked Joan.

"Yes I do very much, it lifts my spirits and makes me feel really good to come here and see you."

"Well if you start feeling too good I'll send you down to Dr. West's office and let him give you my chemo, that will make you feel really bad." Martha told Joan with a gleam in her eye.

Joan laughed and shook her head, "Martha you just won't do, you know Dr. West isn't holding a gun to your head, you can stop taking that chemo any time you want to."

"No, if I don't keep taking the chemo I'll die," Martha replied.

"Is that what you think Martha? That the chemo is going to keep you alive?" Joan asked Martha. Joan was concerned that Martha did not realize how sick she was and why Dr. West had placed her in hospice. She was only getting chemotherapy to help with pain and symptom control, not for it's ability to stop her cancer. Martha had not accepted the fact that she was not going to live much longer. This made Joan's job as a hospice nurse more difficult as Martha would not allow her to help with any plans for her quickly approaching and inevitable decline. Although Dr. West had told Martha the extent of her illness she was not hearing it. Joan tried to explain to Martha that her cancer was not going away but all Martha would say was that she felt like she was getting better. Joan attributed the feeling of Martha getting well to her improved living conditions. Joan tried without success to convince Martha of this fact.

"He doesn't know everything," Martha told Joan when she reflected Dr. West's words.

Joan and Rose sat in the garden after Joan had examined Martha. "I'm very worried about her, I don't know what her relationship is with God and I don't want her to die without accepting Him into her life," Rose told Joan. "I've tried to talk to her but she is in such denial that she blows me off and says for me not to worry about it."

"Since you don't feel like you can get through to her why don't we get some help from Francis?"

"I'm sure she doesn't know how sick Martha is either," Rose said, referring to Martha's closest living relative, her niece. And so it was decided that Rose would call Francis that afternoon to let her know what was going on. Joan said her good byes to Rose and made an appointment to see Martha first thing the next morning.

As Joan entered Martha's room the next day she knew something had drastically changed. Martha was still in bed and Rose was sitting by her side in the white rocker, she had dark circles under her eyes and Joan knew she had not slept well. "What's going on?" Joan asked.

Rose explained the night in explicit detail. "I heard her getting out of bed around two o'clock, she was confused and frightened, she says she didn't fall but I heard a loud thud like she did. I came in here and she was very confused. I couldn't get her to tell me what was wrong but I know she was frightened about something. I got her calmed and stayed with her. She began to clear up a little as the sun came up, and I got her to sit at the table and have some toast and coffee. She told me that she felt the presence of her mother 'near', she hasn't seen her or talked to her, but she feels that her mother is here, somewhere close. She said she had to get ready to go, but she didn't know where she was going."

Joan explained to Rose, "Martha may be experiencing an angel visit. I've been told by other patients and nurses in hospice that angels tend to begin their visits with the dying a week before death. Sometimes sooner. These visits come in the shape of some-one close to the patient, who has died before them, some even say they see the Lord. She may stare off and talk to someone you don't see. You just know she isn't talking to you."

"Yes, I've seen her do that," Rose thoughtfully replied.

Joan reviewed Martha's medications and called to update Martha's doctor. She sat with Martha while Rose went to the local pharmacy to obtain medication, partly to observe Martha, and partly to give Rose a few minutes out. Martha woke up, she smiled when she realized that Joan was there. "How are you Martha?" Joan asked her.

"Oh, I'm not so sure. I had a rough night." Joan helped Martha sit up on the bedside. She helped Martha get up into her favorite chair. Joan drew bath water and helped Martha into the tub. As she assisted Martha wash the places she couldn't easily reach Joan noticed how cancer and age had ravished Martha's body. Martha's skin was as thin as parchment paper and her ribs were prominent. Joan could have counted them from across the room. Martha's hair was sparse due to chemotherapy treatments. She was small, weak, and very thin. It was as though she had been in a long, losing war against disease and time.

Once Martha was safe back in her chair Joan retrieved Martha's lunch from the kitchen and set it up for her to eat.

Martha was, as always, grateful. "I don't know what I would do without you two," she said, speaking of Joan and Rose. "I'll just call you my two angels, but you don't look like that an-gel I saw last night." Rose, who had just walked into the room, stopped dead in her tracks.

"You saw an angel last night?" Joan encouraged Martha to continue.

"Yeah… she was dressed in white and she came flying down from that corner of the ceiling and sat in that chair right over there, looking at me."

"Did she speak?" Joan asked.

"No, she just looked at me." Was the reply, and Martha began eating.

Outside the room Rose said to Joan, "The glory bound train is coming and she is getting on it. And we have to get her ready."

"Rose, I know that's what you want, but what does Martha want for herself?" Joan asked her.

Rose looked out the window as she searched for her answer. "I know, I would be OK if I only knew she was right with her spirituality, but she won't talk about it with me, I don't know why."

Joan looked back at Martha as she left. Martha, smiling, in that rocker, in that room was, Joan thought, the most beautiful thing she would see that day.

The next day Martha showed even more drastic changes. Joan had Rose call her family in. When Joan arrived, Francis was by her bedside and Robert, Francis's husband, and a physician, was examining Martha. He was telling her that he thought she was dying. Martha was crying, as were Francis and Rose. Joan silently placed her arm around Rose and handed her tissues from her pocket. "She saw her mother last night and she talked to her this time, her mother told her it is time to go," Rose informed Joan.

When Robert left the room to confer with Martha's physician Joan sat down close by Martha and took her left hand. Martha's hand was soft and small and much more delicate than Joan's. Joan noticed a small gold band with a ruby stone on the fourth finger. Martha had once told Joan it was the birthstone for July, the birth month of Francis, whom she loved as her own daughter. Martha had never married or had children, and Francis had given her the ring on mother's day some years ago.

Then Joan looked directly into Martha's eyes. She noticed that Martha somehow looked much more tired today, as though her body was telling her it was time to stop fighting this disease. "Martha," Joan began to probe, almost timidly, "Are you at peace with your maker?"

Martha sighed as if she knew why Joan had asked her that, and although she didn't want to think about it she answered a simple, "Yes." Joan did not want to press for more information at that time, she knew Martha was tired and needed to rest. She looked to be sure Rose had heard the conversation. Rose was behind Joan, her arms folded, when Joan turned around Rose forced a smile through her tears.

That was the last time Joan talked with Martha. When

she arrived at the family care center the next day Martha was in a deep non-arousable sleep. Her vital signs had changed and she was actively dying. But she looked like a queen. Rose had so lovingly bathed her and dressed her in beautiful silk pajamas. She laid among spring pattern percale sheets and had on a touch of makeup and cologne. Rose sat by her bed and held her hand. For the entire day Rose dedicated all of her time to Martha's needs. Rose never left Martha's side until she died late that afternoon.

Looking at them reminded Joan of the story from the Bible. How the body of Jesus was so lovingly prepared for burial by Joseph who bargained for His body. There was a silence through out the family care center, as if each resident were waiting with Rose.

Joan sat close to Rose and placed her left arm around Rose's back and shoulder. Joan's right hand passed the tissues to Rose. "She finally told me she saw Jesus and she knows she is going to heaven," Rose said to Joan.

"This is the essence of love," Joan said. "Dying with dignity, surrounded by love. This is how everyone deserves to die. Rose, I wish I could clone you, and show the world that such love exists today. You are the picture of humanity, you are what hospice is all about." Rose smiled and kissed Martha, and ever so gently touched her hair.

That evening the weather was cool. As Joan took her evening walk, she stopped to watch mallards land and swim on Mr. Price's pond about a mile from her home. She leaned against a cedar post and placed her hands on top of it with her chin on her hands. 'So effortlessly they glide along... so beautiful', Joan thought, 'Everything in nature, touched only by the hands of God is so beautiful'. Her eyes were drawn to the sky above the pond. The layers of red just above the pond, outlined by orange under yellow, which faded into a deep dark blue, gave Joan the most peaceful feeling, as the evening sun sat in the western sky behind it all. Then suddenly, the lone sound of a single mallard calling and descending upon the pond to take his place with the others, took Joan's attention from the sky. A year ago she would have missed this scene. She would never have been out here at this time of day to drink it all in. She took a deep cleansing breath before turning for home, grateful for the ability to enjoy such a majestic moment.

Going through Martha's death had a strange effect on Joan. Perhaps it was hospice in general. Looking into Martha's eyes and asking about her spiritual needs had caused a strange twinge in her stomach. She wondered if Martha could see it. If she were going to continue asking people that question she needed to discover what her own spirituality was all about. Although her faith was stronger than ever, she felt the need to make a deeper commitment. She decided to attend classes that her priest was starting on Thursday, for anyone who wanted to learn more about the Bible and Catholicism.

The classes began as she had expected they would. But as time went on, Joan found them quite enjoyable. The priest teaching the classes was very skilled and Joan was amazed by his understanding of family life. He used his memories of his childhood to help them understand his messages.

It took about six weeks for Father Wren to get to the part in his classes when he spoke of marriage vows and relationships between man and wife. Joan could not believe how the seventy six year old priest explained things. She was surprised by how modern his thinking was. Joan came home after her sixth lesson with Father Wren and found James sitting on the couch, reading the newspaper.

"Have I got news for you!" she announced as she sat down beside him. "You know how Father Wren always tells us God wants us to have life and have it in abundance?" Joan asked James.

"Yes," he replied.

She smiled, raised her eyebrows, and continued, "Well that's not all we married couples are supposed to have in abundance."

James put the paper down and smiled at his wife. Joan had raised his interest "Tell me more," he urged her.

Joan told him all about her class that night. She explained how easily Father Wren had taught the class about marriage and the seriousness of that relationship. She explained that she had never thought of sex as the "rewards of marriage," as Father Wren had put it.

Continuing in classes and making an official commitment

to her church and God helped Joan discover what she was all about. She was soon able to look other patients in the eye and ask if they were at peace with their maker more easily, because she had no doubt about her own spiritual relationship with her maker.

SEVEN

"I'm going to quit this job, quit nursing, throw away my stethoscope, tear up my nursing license and go to the college and sign up for the interior decorating course. Then I'm going to buy a little red sports car with a convertible top and ride around all day in it and care about no one... Yep, some day, that's what I'm going to do. But right now I'm going to have a coke, some aspirin and something chocolate." Joan started her car and pulled onto the highway. She had just met Jason Park, a tall young man of seventeen.

Jason was thin, with dark hair and eyes. He had a most charming smile, and a cool mannerism. He had just told Joan that he, "Was not, contrary to popular belief, dying of cancer or anything else," and he, "Did not need any hospice nurse around in the way." Whatever had upset him, he let Joan have it all, full force.

Jason had been diagnosed with leukemia when he was six years old. He had been in and out of remission two times. Although the cancer had taken it's toll he had always managed to rebound with a positive outlook. However, too much time had lapsed since his last remission and the doctors at Children's Hospital had prepared he and his family for the worse. He had been referred to hospice because his oncologist was concerned about his mental state. He had just finished a very intense round of therapy and his body could not withstand any more intensive treatment. Jason was not expected to be well enough to return to Children's for more therapy.

Before Joan could see him again she retrieved his medical records from the hospital and consulted with the social worker who had worked with Jason and his family for years at the hospital. As she poured over his records she realized that she was going to have to find a way of relating to him. She felt sick at first, because her oldest son was the same age as Jason. She had to be able to be objective if she was going to help this young man at the hardest time of his life. Joan made an appointment with Mike and had two bereavement sessions before she could go back to see Jason again.

The second time she saw him was a little more civilized. She told Jason, "Look, it's easy to see how angry you are and you have every right to be angry. All I'm going to do for a few weeks is take your vital signs and review your medications with you. I'll be here if you get sick and need me. I'll keep your doctors at Children's aware of any changes in your condition. When, and if, you are ready to talk to me about anything, I'm here." Jason agreed to these terms of their relationship. He was still not happy to see her but he wasn't hostile either.

Joan was very matter-of-fact when she visited Jason. His mother, Marian, observed their first few visits but eventually she let Joan work with Jason one on one. One hot summer day Jason was not up when Joan arrived, Marian led Joan through the house to his room. It was a typical teenage room. Clothes lined the top of his desk and at least three pairs of shoes were in the middle of the floor. But what caught Joan's eye was the art work. Pencil drawings of sporting events. Pastels of different ball players, and one oil painting of Michael Jordan adorned the young man's room. Jason peered out from under the covers at Joan, and groaned.

"Who's the artist?" Joan was still visually canvassing the art as she asked.

"Oh... me." Came the groggy reply from under the quilt.

Joan's head fell forward and she stopped her mouth from dropping open. "They're beautiful, I had no idea you are such a gifted artist Jason," she replied.

"Well, when you spend half your life in quiet time because you are too sick to walk, you have a lot of time to develop those talents."

It was the first time Joan had found anything personal she could talk to Jason about. She excused herself so he could prepare for her to examine him. Marian told Joan that she was very worried about Jason, he had not been feeling good for a day or two.

After Joan examined Jason she felt more relieved. He had a cough and some chest congestion but Joan didn't feel that it was anything serious. She called the doctor and got orders for an antibiotic and called the prescription into the local pharmacy for Marian to pick up later.

"I told Mom it was nothing to worry about, maybe she'll relax now that you told her the same thing," Jason told Joan.

"Does she do that a lot?" Joan asked him.

"She does now that you are here, you know the big hospice nurse. I think she looks at you as some kind of death angel."

"Maybe I need to get her some help with that. We can't have her driving you crazy with over concern now can we?" Joan smiled at Jason.

"I just want everyone to act like they used to, I don't want them treating me like some kind of invalid. My Mom gets hysterical over every little cough, my Dad avoids me as much as possible, he doesn't know what to say, and my Grandpa cries every time he looks at me."

"That's not good for you Jason. If there is anything you don't need now it is to have to feel guilty over the sadness of others all the time. Have you told them how you feel?" Joan asked him.

"No," Jason responded.

"Well then, do you mind if I talk to them about it?" Joan looked him square in the eye so he couldn't escape the issue.

"Be my guest," Jason replied.

This permission gave Joan the courage to continue. "Jason have any of your friends been coming around, to spend time with you?"

"Yeah, they come over every few days actually. It was hard for them at first but they are coming over more regularly now, and they call after school." Joan was relieved to hear that.

"Do they know about me and hospice?" Joan asked.

"No, I am afraid that will scare them off, so I haven't

mentioned it. I don't want them avoiding me too," Jason was honest with her.

"Oh, I see," was all Joan said in reply.

Joan said good-bye to Marian and not much more at that time. She wanted to talk to Laura and Mike before she said anything to his parents about what Jason had told her. She felt that she had to be especially careful in her dealings with Jason. He had just begun to trust her a little and she wouldn't compromise that for anything.

Joan called the college and spoke to the art instructor about any starving artist shows that might be coming up soon. She found out that something called a "crawl" was held monthly in Charlotte. It was a chance for artists to exhibit their talents and possibly sell some of their work. But mostly, they could meet other artist. There was also the local Fall Festival of Arts, being planned at that time. That event would take place in late October. Joan had informed Jason of both events with enthusiasm that he didn't seem to share.

On one of her visits in early June, Joan had asked Jason what he would like to do with his time. She had asked him to think about it. Today she would ask for his answer. He had shown very little change in his over all condition and he was doing a little more now than sitting in front of the television playing video games and feeling sorry for himself.

"So, Jason, what plans do you have for yourself?" she asked him.

"You mean with the time I have left don't you?" Joan didn't answer him, she just stared and felt a twinge in her stomach. He had actually put much more thought into it than Joan had expected. She was surprised when he began to answer.

"Actually, if I could, I would like to do two things. I'd like to attend the crawl and I'd like to finish high school."

Joan was excited when she heard the word crawl, because she believed he could do that. However, she hoped her shoulders did not visible slump when he said he wanted to finish high school.

He continued, "I feel like the fall festival of arts is a little too high brow for me."

Although Jason had worked hard with a tutor all along

to keep up with his classmates he still had a whole year of school to go, Joan didn't know if he had that much time.

"Do you think it's possible? Do you think I can graduate? I don't want one of those phony honorary diplomas. I want a real diploma, something for my parents to have. It will be my gift to them. I want them to have it to hold, something they can feel and touch. A visible sign to them that all they gave to me counted. Something they can look at and say that I accomplished something, that I made a mark on the world." It was the first time Joan had heard Jason talk about his illness like there was going to be an end to his life at some point. It was a significant event in her eyes. The point when a terminally ill person admits to himself and openly acknowledges the seriousness of his situation to another is a milestone. Then, and only then, can all the work be done that hospice staff need to do.

"Let's talk to the principal. I'll see what I can find out. How many credits do you lack?" Joan asked.

"I need six classes I think. Then I'd have enough to meet minimum graduation requirements," Jason informed Joan.

"Do you have to go full time?" Joan had so many questions.

"No, I think I can go half days."

Then she asked the loaded question, "Have you talked to your parents about this?" Of course he hadn't. When you are the parent of a teenager, you're not often the first to know what is going through their heads. Joan knew what was coming next, the thought had just raced through her head when it came out his mouth.

"Will you tell them for me?" Jason asked.

"No Jason, I can't do that. But I will be here when you tell them if you want me to." She offered him a compromise.

Jason shook his head, he understood. His dad had just pulled up into the driveway, "Well, no time like the present."

"O.K. kid I'm behind you all the way," was Joan's response, and she followed him into the kitchen where his dad and mom were standing.

"Mom, Dad I have something to discuss with you... "Jason began, and told them his plans.

Jason's parents took the news pretty well. They had always supported him. Marian stated, "I admire your determination and strength, I always have. Your personality is what has gotten us through all this. My only concern is whether or not you will be up to the schedule." She looked at Joan for insight. Jason's dad decided to make an appointment for the three of them to meet with the school guidance counselor the next day.

Joan told Jason "I would quite enjoy seeing what a real live crawl is all about, would you mind if I join you in that adventure?"

"Sure," Jason agreed. Jason was to invite his friends and they would set out to sell art the next Friday evening at five.

On her way to her next visit Joan wondered if Jason had chosen to finish school as a bargaining attempt. Did he think that by choosing a long range goal he would some how be able to delay his fate as long as possible? She made an appointment with Mike to discuss Jason's case that afternoon.

When she sat down to a late lunch with Mike she was not startled by anything he had to tell her. "Jason's dad has talked to me about how angry he is that his son is going to die so young. He is seeing Jason's life through his own eyes. He has graduated from high school, college, fallen in love, and taken his place in the work force. He has a family and has lived forty some years. He is angry that Jason is not going to have the same opportunities he has been given. He feels guilty that he has lived so much longer than Jason is going to."

"It helped him to understand that teenagers don't see the world quite the same way. A year is an eternity to them. Long range goals and plans are different. For a seventeen year old young man, finishing high school very often is long range planning. I told him that Jason would not mourn the loss of all those social climbing events because they were not yet important in his life. I explained that Jason would mourn the loss of his high school diploma if he could not obtain that goal, because it was where Jason had chosen to focus his attention. Jason is more likely to mourn the loss of his friends and his role in their lives than the loss of any future family he has not yet planned to have."

"Laura has worked with Marian and helped her understand that her teenage son can not live in an environment where she is overly anxious. Marian has chosen to seek medical advise and counseling for her own anxiety and is coping better over all. At least she is learning to force smiles whenever Jason is around, even if she is crying on the inside." Mike finished speaking and the two ate quietly, each deep in their own thoughts.

Joan broke the silence. "I am pleased to hear that so much social work has been done so soon with this family. Thank you Mike for all of your hard work. I am going with Jason, Marian and some of his friends to Charlotte to an art crawl."

Mike wanted to respond but didn't know how to say what he felt. "Oh, how interesting," he finally said. "But I don't envy you." They laughed and asked for their check.

Joan had asked for a short day on Friday so she could meet Jason and his friends early and head out to the crawl. As she neared his large country home she almost missed his drive. The sight of a group of six teenagers sitting on and standing around a picnic table in a yard caught her off guard. To look at the sight one would never know the significance of the event. Marian was ready to go, camera and all. "Mom, I'm not sure you take pictures at one of these things, and I think you're way over dressed." Jason mused.

"Oh, it'll be fine let's just go." Marian retorted.

Jason's friends loaded several of his drawings in Joan's car and the group managed to pile into two cars. Each car with one adult driver, much to the disappointment of the teens. After what seemed a short six hours, Jason and his friends decided they had had enough of the art world and the group headed for home. Jason had sold three drawings.

The crawl was the topic of conversation between Joan and Jason until school started the second week of August.

Through negotiations Jason had managed to get a short day schedule. He would take three classes each semester and if he passed everything he would have just enough credits to meet graduation requirements.

"You don't have to make the honor roll, just pass, a C is good enough," Marian had told him the night before the first day of class.

"Mom, go take your temperature, you must be sick!" Jason gave her a surprised look.

The first weeks of school went well. Jason was able to

attend classes regularly. His principal had sent home notices to the families of the other children relaying the message that there was a student in the school who was immunocompromised and could not be exposed to other students who had chicken pox or certain other viruses. He had asked that the school be notified of all such cases immediately so that Jason's parents could be instructed if he was exposed. Joan met with the school nurse and asked that she be notified if there were any viral or influenza outbreaks at school. She instructed Jason that it would be best if he stayed home during such times.

"Yeah, yeah, yeah... I know the drill," he replied to her overprotection of him.

Whether Jason was determined to make this work, or because he was exhausted Marian noticed that he always took a long nap after school. She never questioned him, she just kept her loving eye on him. Marian tried hard to boost his energy reserves with her meal planning. She served lots of vegetables and packed his coat pockets with fresh fruit. She knew when he was away he was going to eat burgers and pizza but she had to help where she could.

Jason stayed on his medicines as prescribed and took lots of vitamins his friends had gotten for him at the health food store. Joan continued to visit him once a week and monitored him closely. Except for a few minor colds she could find very little changes in his over all condition. In fact being back with his classmates seemed to have a very therapeutic effect on Jason overall. It had been a long time since he had been able to attend school with such regularity. He enjoyed not being a patient for a change. He had even been on a few dates with Stephanie Rogers, a beautiful girl his own age.

Marian and Bob received a call from Children's Hospital in early October. They wanted to check Jason. They requested that he make an appointment with his oncologist and plan to spend most of the day there. "O.K., we'll do it," Bob said as the secretary gave them an appointment for December sixteenth, the first day of Christmas break, for Jason. He could not understand why he had to go back to Children's, since they had told them that there was nothing else they could do. "And besides we have Joan here if we need any thing."

However, Joan interjected. "Oh no, I am not a stand in for your doctor. If he says he needs to see you, then you should go." Her voice was half defensive and half demanding.

It was not a peaceful wait for anyone. Jason had been a little rebellious, becoming argumentative about his routines. However, now that he was actually in the car, Jason had time to reflect on what he would tell the doctors when they told him he still had but a short time to live. He would inform them that he had no choice but to live until June first when he would receive his diploma.

After what seemed an endless battery of blood tests and scans Jason was finished and allowed to go home. He would come back after the holidays to meet with Dr. Wong. "I can hardly wait," he told the receptionist who handed him the appointment card.

Christmas was bitter sweet at the Park household that year. Everyone tried to make the best of the holiday but they were keenly aware that it would be Jason's last. The hospital visit had made Jason depressed, but his friends kept him entertained and he soon found himself enjoying the holiday.

Christmas had never been more sweet at the McRae household. Joan was experiencing a peace that she had never known before. This Christmas was very special to her. It was the first time she really meant it when she said she didn't care if she received any gifts. She felt that the whole year had been her gift. The patients had showered her with gifts. She was embarrassed by it from time to time. She told Faye as she entered the office on December twenty-third, "Hospice is a strange place at Christmas, I wish they wouldn't do this. They are so good to me when I go into their homes, that is enough."

Faye just smiled and said she understood.

Midnight Mass that year was the most beautiful one Joan had ever seen. Each ritual was special, she felt as if she had never truly attended the celebration before, at least not in the truest spirit of the season. Although she was on call that Christmas, it was quiet. This was typical, since many, many hospice patients' goal is to live through Christmas. She only answered a few questions. She thanked God that none of the patients died on that day. It is too hard for those who remain behind, she thought, to

55

have each and every Christmas from now on to be a conflict between the happiest and the saddest day of the year. Joan thought it would be too hard to bear.

The holiday season ended peacefully and quietly and Joan returned to work on December twenty-eighth to find a message on her voice mail from Marian. It sounded urgent and asked her to call as soon as possible.

"Hi Marian, what's up?" Joan waited nervously for the reply.

"We got a call this morning from Dr. Wong, he wants to see Jason today if possible. So, we won't be here for your visit."

"O.K. well, drive carefully and I'll see you first thing in the morning if that's all right. Eight o'clock?" Joan asked Marian.

Marian assured her that would work for them and Joan changed her schedule, clearing time for them the next day.

The day was long for Joan. She worried about Jason and found him on her mind all day. Even though she went about her route and office work she couldn't shake the gnawing feeling from her stomach. She slept poorly that night and sprung from the bed when the alarm sounded, causing James to ask her what was wrong. She assured him, "I'm just concerned for one of my patients. It will all work out by the end of the day." She kissed his cheek before hurrying off to work.

Joan arrived at the Park home exactly at eight. She could tell when she walked in that something even more difficult than they were already going through was happening.

"Oh, good morning Joan," Marian welcomed her friend in, "What about some coffee?" And even though Joan usually didn't take patients up on these offers she did this time. She felt like she needed it.

She walked by Jason and tapped the brim of his baseball cap with her hand, "Hey boy, you speaking to me today?"

"Hey, hey, hey, the hair, the hair… careful," Jason's sense of humor was still intact, that made Joan more at ease. She did her usual routine examination while Marian finished getting coffee. Marian returned to the den as Joan finished.

"O.K., I can't stand it another minute," was what Joan wanted to say, but she settled for a more reserved approach, "How did your visit go yesterday?" And as soon as Marian sat down she began to answer.

"I'm not too sure. I'm a little confused by it, I hope you can explain it better. I have the greatest respect for Dr. Wong but I can't always understand what he says. He wants Jason to consider more short term treatment with chemotherapy, and maybe, bone marrow transplant. And they think his body is trying to go into remission. They found leukemia in small amounts in just a few places where they think that if they go ahead and treat it now Jason has a good chance for a total remission. What do you think?" Marian asked Joan.

Joan was stunned, "Well, I knew Jason has remained stable for a much longer period than I had expected but I've kept waiting for the decline to begin again. When Jason was admitted to hospice he was very worn from all the intensive treatments, two years of intense therapy had left his body too weak to recover quickly. But everyone has taken so many measures to assure his success in finishing school that we've been given more than we had hoped for," was the only explanation Joan had to offer Marian and Jason.

"Jason, what do you think about all this?" Joan was eager to hear his thoughts.

"Well," Jason began, more serious now. "I'm not sure. I went through so much pain and pure agony before, and if I get down like that again, I think it will be harder for me to get back up this time. I would like to dream of a remission but I'm not sure I can. I hope it doesn't sound like I'm ungrateful to God or the doctors or anything I just would hate to only have six months left, and have to spend it in the hospital."

Joan told him, "I understand." She agreed to check with his doctor and look at all his labs and x-ray reports and see if she could come up with any more information which would be of help to them. She made an appointment to see them in three days.

Joan wasn't much clearer of her own impression of Jason's prognosis after she had seen all his lab and x-ray results than she was before. She had spoken to Dr. Wong and understood that he wanted to try short term therapy on Jason. He knew that Jason was not up to long term therapy but felt that short term intensive therapy now could keep Jason's leukemia at a low level longer or could totally stop it. He had stopped therapy before because he could see that Jason's body just couldn't endure any more.

"I was shocked to say the least when I saw Jason and his test results. And I have found a bone marrow donor match if Jason will come." Dr. Wong went on to explain that the therapy Jason had been given had apparently worked after some time passed, because the boy he had seen in the office was not the same one he discharged to hospice six months earlier. "Children never cease to amaze me," he told Joan.

Joan asked the busy physician one more question, whether for Jason's sake or for hers, she had to know the answer. "What are his chances for a long term or total remission in percentages with this treatment? So I can understand."

The doctor was positive, "I'd say about ninety percent." Joan breathed rapidly and with excitement she thanked Dr. Wong for his time. She was estatic for Jason.

Joan met with Jason and his family and told them everything that Dr. Wong had told her. The treatment would be brief and the teachers housed at the hospital would work to help Jason keep up with his school studies. Joan would discharge him from hospice while he received this aggressive therapy.

Then Joan gave them the most coincidental news. "Oh, by the way, Mrs. Duncan, the school nurse, doesn't think you should attend classes the next two weeks, flu outbreak, lots of your friends have been at their doctors offices during the holiday break too." Everyone laughed, a nervous forced laugh, but the comic relief was welcomed, and they all felt better for it.

After a brief discussion Jason turned to Joan and asked, "What do you think I should do?"

Joan had hoped he wouldn't do that. She knew too much. She knew the emotional drain they were already undergoing. She knew that his parents had had previous arguments with his insurance company. She was a little skeptical that his chances of a total remission with only short term therapy was as good as she had been told.

Then Joan looked at Jason. She looked at his big doe eyes, his youthful body. She stared into the face of innocence. And all she could see was that he was only seventeen years old, and nothing else mattered. "I think you should go back, I think you should fight, at least one more time. Then you will know you did all you could and you won't have to wonder."

Joan discharged Jason from hospice that day. He entered Children's Hospital the following Monday to begin treatment. Joan called him a few times after that to see how he was getting along. The treatment left him weak and he was working hard to rebuild his body, but it was difficult. He worked on his school work the best he could. He took his mother up on her offer to maintain only barely passing grades. Stephanie visited him daily once he was home, and helped as much as she could. She wrote several term papers for him when he was too weak to do it. She just signed his name and felt absolutely no guilt for it. Joan went by to see him when her schedule allowed.

Joan received an envelope in the mail from Jason in February. It was a pastel of an angel carrying a lamp. Jason explained that it reminded him of her because she had helped lead him out of his own darkness. He asked her to share it with the others. Joan had it framed and it became part of the hospice office. Mike had a plaque made which he had mounted below the art work.

In May Joan received one more gift from Jason. An invitation to his commencement exercise. Joan stood with Marian and Bob in the crowd of over one thousand people. And her eyes were no dryer than anyone else's during the standing ovation, as Jason Marcus Park walked across the stage, shook hands with the principal and received his diploma from City High School.

How the Golden Retriever Got His Golden Fur
Printed with permission of the author: Sean Summer

A long time ago God gave Earth light so all things could see. There was a dog in a nearby village. He was happy to see and feel the warmth of the sun. Then he saw that his fur was black with some gray on it, he didn't want black fur. The dog so admired the sun that he wanted fur that was golden like the sun. He made plans to go to the highest mountain he could find and speak to God.

That night he went to the mountain of God, and saw a golden light. He set one paw on the mountain and a voice boomed out of the light of gold, "Come ol' faithful one! Come and seek your true self!" The dog climbed the mountain of God, and when he came to the top he saw a faithful face dressed in a white robe with a golden rope around the hip. God asked, "What is your wish black creature?"

The dog replied, "I wish that I could be a Golden dog, like the sun, ol' God."

God put one hand on the golden rope, took it off, and put it on the dog. Then he said with a smile on his face, "There you go, and you shall be called the Golden Retriever, because of your golden fur. And you too will shine like the sun."

After that the dog was happy for the rest of his life. When he died God sent him to the sun. That is how the Golden Retriever got it's beautiful fur.

EIGHT

Joan thought the winter of 1997 was the coldest one she had ever seen. At least until she discovered how the other nurses endured the weather. "Long Johns, honey," Rae told her, "You have to buy yourself some thermal underwear." Joan added that to the list of one hundred and one things they didn't tell her in orientation.

The nurses were sitting in the office on a typical Friday afternoon. That's the day they all tried to take back any comp time they had coming and head out early. When the familiar music came on, Rae turned to Joan and said, "You know what I think of when I hear this song these days?" Joan shook her head and the smile was already beginning before Rae opened her mouth and sung new words to the old familiar tune. "Death Angel, Death Angel will you be mine? Death Angel, Death Angel I need you all the time." The song made heads turn, mouths smile, and computers stop through out all the office.

"You are seriously deranged," Joan told Rae.

"Well you don't have to be crazy to work like this but it helps." Joan laughed, told her friend good bye and headed out of the office to see Tom Davis before she went home for the weekend.

The weather had turned colder and the clouds were moving out, which was a good sign to Joan because Tom's breathing was worse on cloudy wet days. Joan had hopes of changing some medications and getting his anxiety under better control so he could have a good weekend. 'And so could the call nurse', Joan

61

thought as she neared Tom's home and pulled into his drive. Tom's house was an older house in the historic district of town. Beautiful yes, but damp when the weather was humid.

Tom sat in his easy chair. He was always dressed the same way. First in his clothes, which always included a heavy weight flannel shirt. His gray sweater covered that. Then he was wrapped in his brown blanket. The heat in the house was warm enough but he couldn't breathe if it was, "suffocatingly hot." His hair was thick and silver like ice frozen to naked tree branches on a cold winter day. It matched his wire rimmed glasses.

Tom had retired from Southern Railroad some twenty years earlier. He was five foot ten. He had large hands and a gentle manner.

Tom was having a restless day. He was close to death and his family was well prepared. Joan sat on a tapestry stool in front of Tom watching his breathing. She had disguised her actions by telling him she needed to trim his fingernails. The big gray and white male cat on the chair arm caught her attention. She had seen him before when she came to see Tom, but he was always skittish and ran away from her to hide in a safe place, where he chose to stay until she left. Joan would always believe that there was a special relationship between God and animals.

It was as if animals had a special command from the Master that people didn't always recognize or appreciate. She had witnessed a special bond between her grandmother and the small Pomeranian, that was her constant companion after the death of her husband. The dog didn't eat right for a year after her death, and kept going to her bed to look for her.

Once when Joan's youngest son, Brad, was very ill, following surgery, his Siamese cat laid by his side purring and meowed only if someone else approached the boy as if to say, "Can't you see he doesn't feel well." The cat scolded Joan relentlessly as she changed Brad's wound dressings daily.

Joan had witnessed this bond when she worked in a nursing home where a salvaged greyhound had been adopted by the residents to live among them. An elderly woman fell and laid on the floor, unable to get up due to a broken hip. The dog immediately heard the loud sound of her hitting the tile floor. He ran through the crowded hall of people, as gracefully as a deer retreating into the woods from the sight of hunters. Weaving first one way and then another, around other residents without touching them, until he reached her side. He barked to signal to the staff that she needed help, and snuggled her. He never left her until she was placed on the gurney by the emergency medical technicians, and carried onto the elevator. He was her reason for recuperating, for she worried about who would give him his evening meal, a job that was hers. As soon as she could speak after surgery she told the doctors she had to get well and go home to take care of her hero.

"I don't know what is wrong with him," Joan heard Angie, Tom's wife of forty years say. The sound jolted her back to reality. "He almost never comes in here. Today I can't get him to go out. He has been in here all of today and yesterday." Joan watched the cat as he crept close to Tom's side and positioned himself where he could get a clear view of the formal dining area. That's where Tom said they were. All the people that Angie and Joan couldn't see. For they were not in Tom's privileged position.

Tom had asked Angie several times that day, "What are all those people doing in there?"

"What people, there are no people here except you and me?" she had replied.

"Can't you see them, there are at least fifteen, in there," Tom insisted, pointing to the formal dining room through his bedroom doors. "I can't believe you can't see them too." Angie, seeing he was becoming agitated with her, let the subject drop.

But Joan knew what was happening. She had seen this many times before. She even knew what the cat was doing in that room. As she watched him look at his beloved master, then stretch his head out to see if they were still there, Joan knew he saw them too, and that they concerned him. He stayed close, keeping a watch over his master in these, his final hours.

Joan had first seen this when the elder schnauzer, which belonged to a thirty five year old master would not leave her bed the day she died. He stayed in bed with her and snuggled as close as possible. He never barked or made one sound. He would not eat nor would he drink the whole day. He had to be taken by force from her side to go out for a bathroom break. He shivered the entire time and cried until he was finally escorted back inside. As soon as he was released from his leash he ran back to his rightful place at her side where he could keep a watch over her. It was his right as man's best friend.

One night Joan had been called to the home of Deanna, a beautiful young woman who told her "Nurse, I'm ready to go now, I'm tired." She noticed a small white poodle under the bed. Joan asked the family members if the dog had been acting strange that day.

They seemed surprised that Joan knew that. "Yes, he never comes in here but today we can't get him out, and he keeps looking up over the bed, it's as though he sees something." Joan didn't respond, but she knew he did see something. He saw the angels waiting to take their loved one. That was what Joan had come to believe.

Once, Joan watched while she waited for one of her patients to die. The family had called her to be with them that night. She watched as two family cats walked silently, repeatedly passed his bedroom. They looked up over the bed, then to their master, then over the bed. Joan could only imagine what they saw. Joan had petted one of them. She picked the cat up, took it to the bedside so she could say good bye. The cat gingerly licked his hand and purred. She snuggled in close by his side and gave a slight hiss when she was removed.

Then there was Midnight, a huge, beautiful, black lab. He greeted Joan's Suburban with tail wagging and mouth open demanding her attention when she came to see his owner, Frank. First she had to pet Midnight, then she could attend to Frank. But the only way she could get in her Suburban to leave was to pet Midnight for a few minutes before she left. The day Frank died Midnight laid in the carport and turned neither head nor eye to Joan as she walked right by him to pronounce Frank. "Oh, you poor thing, you look so sad," Joan remarked as she walked past the dog.

But nothing made a more lasting impression on Joan than the day she was on call and went to pronounce Sally, a sweet middle aged woman. Joan was keenly aware of the beautiful boxer dog that kept coming into the room and looking at the bed where she laid. Although the family kept shooing him out Joan explained that he needed to say good bye. He knew something was going

64

on, and probably knew exactly what it was. Joan was in the kitchen when the funeral director arrived and began to take the body out of the house. She heard the dog begin to cry, he sounded like a baby. He cried the whole time that his loving master was being carried from her home. Joan went to him, petted him and apologized for not having allowed him time with her, to say his good byes, before she left.

Yes, Joan knew exactly what the big gray cat saw in Tom's dining room that afternoon. She knew what this ritual was all about. As she told Tom good bye that day she kissed his forehead, squeezed his hand, and bid him farewell. Since she was not on call, she knew she would not see him alive again. As she left the room she looked at the cat, that was silent, alert, and keeping a continuous watch over the man he loved, and the angels who had come to take him away.

NINE

The day was bright and sun reflected off the waters of the lake. Even though it was late February, the temperature was a mild sixty six degrees Fahrenheit. The skies were blue with a few feathery white clouds. It was the kind of day that reminded Joan why she loved being a hospice nurse. As she drove through the country roads she thought again about that red sports car with the convertible top. Although she knew it was totally impractical and doubted she would ever buy it.

Joan pulled into Fred Winslow's drive and began taking in all the sights. The long winding ribbon of white concrete stretched out before her like a welcome mat. It was cornered on either side by large flowering pompous grass, which swallowed the Suburban as Joan turned into the drive. Beautiful weeping willow trees lined the drive to the right and left all the way to the house.

Fred was a wealthy man, Joan thought. His home was on the lake and surrounded by twelve acres of beautiful lake front property. He was a builder by trade and a gardener by design. His home was beautifully landscaped and every where one looked a beautiful flower or plant waited to entertain the senses. Fred knew just what to plant where, and how. Never had a more beautiful home graced the pages of House Beautiful than the day they released a ten page layout of Fred and Gillian Winslow's twenty five hundred square foot tutor.

Joan dismounted her Suburban, took in a deep breath, and started her descent along the glorious stone path to the house.

She always felt like she had been through a walk in the park after she left his garden. Somehow she felt like she should be having a guided tour. She heard the sounds of their voices as she neared the lake front side of the house. Then she saw them. Fred in his boat with his hip waders on. Hat on head, fishing pole in his right hand, left hand on his hip, about ten feet off the pier.

Gillian was on the pier with her camera focused, taking picture after picture as Fred directed. Fred Winslow was laughing as always. Joan shook her head and took a chair where she could watch the two "youngsters" at play. She sat silently trying to blend with the scenery until they were finished, and Fred was satisfied that Gillian had properly caught the 'real' him on film for all his family to remember.

Then she waited some more while Gillian laughed and turned to walk toward her, and Fred put the boat back in the watershed, and tied it to the pier. The pompous grass near Joan almost obscured her from Gillian's view as she tried to refocus her eyes after the sun reflecting off the water had seemed to temporarily blind her.

Gillian spoke to Joan and said, "I'm going to bring a pitcher of tea and a 'to go' cup for you and glasses for me and Fred, from the house. Would you like to come in?" she invited Joan inside. Joan followed her into the house to wash her hands. She knew the routine. It was of no use to reject the glass of tea in her 'to go' cup when it was offered by Gillian. For Gillian was a lady, in every sense of the word, and her home rang with southern hospitality. Joan didn't dare refuse her offer. It would, she was sure, be considered impolite.

By the time Joan had returned back outside Fred was near the picnic table taking off his hip waders. He was a big robust man, at least six foot four, who laughed all the time. He was the happiest patient Joan knew. When he got sick, with end stage cardiac disease, and the doctors told him he had a short time to live, Gillian had asked him what he was going to do, how he was going to get through it. He had assured her that he would accept this challenge like he had accepted every other challenge in his life, with dignity and courage, and always laughter. He had made two rules for Joan's visits. "Always meet with me out by the lake, for that is where I want to spend as much time as possible. And never let me see you frown. I couldn't stand to be around sad people now." Joan tried hard to live up to his expectation.

And laugh they did. It always started the same way. Gillian would bring them both tea and by the time the visit was finished and business was done, the tea was gone and Joan knew another one of Fred's humorous stories, from what seemed to be an endless collection of the best ever told.

One day Joan asked him, "So, looking back what advice would you offer a young person in the world today?"

Fred scowled his face, bit on his lower lip a little and after a short time said, "Laugh often, love well, and enjoy the ride, because it is an awesome adventure if you will only let it be." Even though she didn't realize it at the time those words were to stay with Joan for the rest of her life.

Fred was still in charge of everything. He was still telling everyone what to do instead of delegating things to others. Gillian had some success getting him to slow down by keeping him home more, but not much. Sometimes Joan thought Fred was going just a little overboard with a good thing. Like the day he went to the funeral home to make his own arrangements. He didn't want Gillian 'wasting' too much money on his funeral. "He even asked the funeral director if it cost more to be carried from the church to the graveside in the new Mercedes hertz than in the old Cadillac," Gillian told Joan. "Then after seeing the price of caskets and cemetery plots he decided he needed to be cremated." Gillian was aghast but she knew better than to argue with him when it came to money. She turned to Fred and said, "When you die people are going to say, there goes the stingiest rich man I know!"

To which Fred promptly replied, "No, they'll say there goes the smartest rich man I know!" Joan just kept to her paper work like she was hearing nothing but the mallards playing on the water.

The way they lived, the way they loved, the way they were always so intense was amazing to Joan. It was refreshing to have a light hearted fun visit, and Joan admired the couple. She knew that Fred was putting things in order in his own way, even if it were out of the ordinary for her, it wasn't for him. He was accepting death the way he had accepted life.

68

"I love to ski," he had once told her. "What I'd really love is if someone who was a champion skier would take my ashes to the top of the highest slope at Beech Mountain and open the urn, tilt it, and start skiing down the slope. So my ashes would fall all the way down the mountain and I could be part of it forever."

Joan told him, "I'll see what I can arrange," but he told her never mind.

Gillian had already told him that at that point she would be in charge and it wasn't going to happen. "She wants to keep me around so she's going to keep my ashes in there on the fireplace, and take me out in the boat and sit me out here on sunny days so I can be near the lake. I think she wants to look at me and laugh while she's spending my money," Fred told Joan, nodded his head and winked. "Yeah, I know what she's really all about."

"Yeah well, she knows how you are too," Joan was straight faced with not the slightest hint of a smile as Fred quickly glanced at her.

Fred had offered to take Joan out in the boat during her visits from time to time but she had declined so far, telling him she would when the weather was warm enough. "Oh, we have jackets, you won't freeze," he had chided her. So one afternoon when Joan had a cancellation in her schedule she and Gillian and Fred took the boat to the middle of the lake and drank tea. Joan had been late the day before getting off work so she took some personal time.

They used binoculars to take in the sights of all the beautiful lake front homes. Fred pointed out to Joan who lived in each of the houses and what each person did for a living. "It's easier for robbers to use the lake to break into houses because it is quicker to run away from the police on the water," Fred told her.

"Do you have a lot of privacy here in the summer?" Joan asked.

Gillian answered this time. "Through the summer it can get noisy but during the fall and winter it's generally very quiet. People who live here enjoy the quiet so they keep it down."

It had been a good way to spend a few hours. Joan felt relaxed and refreshed as she climbed back into the Suburban and headed home for the day.

The next Tuesday afternoon Joan returned to the office

just after three thirty. Faye met her as she came in the door. "Joan you have to go to Fred Winslow's home… he just died." Joan's mouth dropped in disbelief.

"No! I just came from there, there must be some mistake."

Faye explained to her, "I know, Gillian just called and stated that you had left their home only a few minutes before. Gillian had returned her serving set to the house. When she returned to the lake side, Fred was asleep in his hammock. Only he wasn't just asleep. When she tried to wake him she couldn't."

Joan attended his memorial service on Friday morning. There were more smiles at the funeral than tears. That is how he would have wanted it. Joan looked at the expensive box Gillian had chosen to place his ashes in. It was of imported mahogany with pure gold trim. "It must have cost a small fortune," Joan whispered under her breath as she stared at the picture of him beside the box, standing in his boat, one hand on this fishing rod, the other on his hip. Then a strange thing happened. Joan started thinking about him and what he would say if he saw that box.

"Look, just look," he would have said, if he could speak. "Look at that box, do you know how much she paid for that box, I bet it cost a lot more than it's worth." Then Joan started laughing, thinking about that box on a pair of skis on the top of Beech Mountain. She laughed so hard she held her hands over her mouth to muffle the sounds. Her face was flushed and mourners at the church came over and patted her on the shoulder because they thought she was crying. That made her laugh even more.

Joan felt like Fred was right there beside her in the pew as she listened to the minister, taking it all in and laughing the whole time about all the expense Gillian had incurred to give him a proper send off. At one time Gillian looked over at Joan and they both smiled. Gillian winked at Joan, then Joan knew that Gillian had chosen that box on purpose, to have the last word, and to share one last laugh, with her beloved husband.

TEN

The March winds blew fierce that morning. As Joan stood on the porch of the large brick home she scanned the neighborhood. Nothing much to see except houses, streets, and a bus stop. After what seemed like an eternity she heard two locks unlocking, and came face to face with Elizabeth Rorie. Elizabeth was twenty nine years old with a seven year old son, Benjamin. She was tall, thin, beautiful... and dying of AIDS. Thus was the reason Joan found herself at Elizabeth's home.

As Joan came to know Elizabeth she found out more about how Elizabeth came to be a hospice patient. Elizabeth had spent most of her life, since she was fifteen, estranged from her family. When she found out how sick she was last year her mother had bade her home so she could take care of Elizabeth and Ben. Elizabeth, grateful for the help, agreed to return home.

Elizabeth accepted hospice positively and Joan enjoyed getting to know her. Although Joan thought she had formed no preconceived ideas of what Elizabeth would be like, she wasn't anything like Joan expected her to be. Although Elizabeth and Joan were different, they were more alike.

Elizabeth had been raised very poor. She was the middle of nine children and her mother, Georgia, was disabled due to an auto accident. Her father did his best, but he was good at working, not childrearing. She had quit school when she was fourteen and began walking the streets. She was heavy into drug use by the time she was fifteen. Joan felt sorry for her because she thought that Elizabeth never really had much of a chance of growing up unscathed by her harsh environment. But Elizabeth never asked for Joan's pity. She was striving to maintain her own dignity. She wanted to stay as beautiful as possible, although the disease fought her the whole way.

The thing that impressed Joan most was Elizabeth's attitude. She never blamed anyone or anything for her illness. She accepted full blame stating, "This is all my fault, I know I did this to myself." She spent her time trying to make arrangements for Ben. He was her only concern. She kept her illness a secret from her community so Ben would not be ridiculed at school. She told him she had cancer. It made Joan sad to think that at a time when Elizabeth was so sick, she couldn't reach out for the help and understanding of those around her, that would have been such a help to her and her family.

This is a cruel disease, Joan thought. She considered how Elizabeth was so isolated from the community. Joan had arranged those services she could through hospice for support for Elizabeth, Ben, and her family. Working for hospice and home health had taught Joan that she couldn't fix everything. Sometimes she had to look at a situation, give what she could, and go on. Joan had to be satisfied with doing the best she could for them. It wasn't always easy. Elizabeth and her family were always appreciative of everything Joan did for them.

Elizabeth talked often about what would become of Ben after she died. She began searching for placement. Elizabeth had made arrangements for Benjamin to be placed in a home with a friend she had met through the county services, and was elated when she told Joan about it. "Maria has adopted several other children and is doing an amazing job with them. With her, Ben will have structure and safety and would be properly raised by a caring gentle hand. Ben has spent time with them and he is happy there."

He told Elizabeth he was excited about having new brothers and a sister. Elizabeth told her mother, "I want Ben to have a chance to forget all this pain." And although Ben loved his grandparents, Elizabeth knew they were not able to raise him.

Laura had become one of Elizabeth's closest confidants. The social worker had invested many hours in helping Elizabeth make her final preparations. One afternoon Laura and Elizabeth sat in the two large white wicker chairs on the front porch of Georgia's home talking.

Laura asked Elizabeth about Ben's father, but she would not disclose his name. "Do you think he should have to pay child support, especially now?" Laura had asked.

Elizabeth lowered her eyes and turned her head away. Laura could see this was difficult for her to talk about. Finally, after what seemed an eternity, Elizabeth answered. "He doesn't know anything about Ben, and I don't want him to know," Elizabeth told Laura. "He's not the kind of person that Ben needs to be spending time with, and besides, he can't take care of himself, let alone take care of someone else. He hasn't contacted me since Ben was born and I'd just as soon keep it that way."

Elizabeth continued, "If anything good can come out of this it is that I am a better person for it, and Ben will have a better life with Maria than I could have given him. Even though I've cleaned up, I still have problems that would have always followed me. Ben doesn't deserve that in his life. He deserves better."

Ben got off the big orange school bus and approached the two women sitting on the porch. Without a word he sat on Elizabeth's lap and gave her a big hug. "Ben and I have had a big talk about this haven't we?" The boy automatically shook his head to show agreement with his mother. "I want Ben to know everything that I go through. I want him to see what living that life-style can lead to. Ben's never going to take drugs are you baby?"

"No mama." he replied. Then he was off, into the house getting ready for homework.

Joan had made weekly visits to Elizabeth's house for two months noting only small changes in her condition. Elizabeth continued losing weight slowly over time. Her appetite wasn't good. Some weeks she slept more than she was awake. Then as if she had awoken refreshed from a good night's sleep, she would greet Joan at the door smiling her old familiar smile. The only notable change was the cane she now used for walking.

Elizabeth's favorite color was yellow, and she loved daffodils. Joan saw sparse flowers planted in her neighborhood. Since one of her other patients lived in the country surrounded by fields of daffodils Joan tried to pick a handful of them to take with her when she went to see Elizabeth. Elizabeth would hold them close to her nose and take a deep breath and hold it for the longest time. She told Joan, "I don't know why, but when I smell butter-cups and close my eyes I have the happiest thoughts." That made it worth the extra ten minutes it took for Joan to stop and pick the flowers.

By the first weeks of summer, Elizabeth had begun to lose ground. She had repeated infections, and her pain was becoming difficult to control. Joan had arranged to have premixed medications delivered which infused by machine. Elizabeth knew she was losing ground. She often called the nurse on call to check her infusion pump. Joan figured out that this was happening more and more often as Elizabeth came closer and closer to death. "Elizabeth, are you afraid?" Joan asked her.

Elizabeth lowered her eyes, "Not during the day but yeah, some times at night I can't sleep."

Although Elizabeth had taken advantage of counseling, and spiritual guidance, Joan let her know it was normal for her to have some fear. And it was normal for her not to talk about it. Joan had noticed that some of her patients do not verbally admit their fear as death nears. Joan began to prepare Georgia and Ben. As the final days approached, Elizabeth stopped drinking except for sips of water, and spoke very few words, usually to Ben. She tired easily but when she did have energy she always wanted Ben to be close by. She still had so much to teach him. She would call him close by the bed and give him all the rules for his future that she was able to give. "Don't quit school, find a way to go to college, save the money from my life insurance, it's not much but it will get you started in college. Always be good and don't ever, ever mess with drugs."

Elizabeth was quite dehydrated one Thursday evening when Joan called Chris to give her call report. "I expect them to call you, I don't think she will make it through the night," she told Chris. Before leaving home on Friday morning Joan called Chris. Chris hadn't heard anything from Elizabeth's family. Joan was surprised by the news.

Joan went by to check on Elizabeth first. Elizabeth was shaking, had a fever, and was in a great deal of pain. Her mother was crying and Ben was rubbing her head. Joan asked Georgia to get her some cool water in a pan that she could use to bathe Elizabeth. She called Chris to help her. Chris arrived shortly after being called and the two worked diligently to try to comfort Elizabeth.

The two nurses were able to get Elizabeth's temperature down, and called the doctor for permission to increase her pain medicine. They were given orders to increase the morphine slowly until pain relief was obtained. By noon, after the two nurses had worked for hours, Elizabeth was resting comfortably. With Ben on her right side holding her hand, and Georgia on her left side stroking her hair Elizabeth looked peaceful. Joan left to see her other patients.

When Joan returned at five o'clock to check on Elizabeth the house was full of family members. Joan could see that Elizabeth was again restless and beginning to moan. Again she called Dr. West and received orders to increase the morphine and add an anti-anxiety medication to help Elizabeth rest better. Again she helped Georgia sponge bathe Elizabeth to cool her off. Joan was glad Ben had tired and was napping in another room. Joan called Beverly, who was on call that Friday and told her what was going on. "I am on call Saturday and if you need me you can call," Joan told Beverly. Joan slept through the night and called Saturday to meet Beverly mid way between their homes to exchange the call box. Beverly informed her that she hadn't heard one word from Georgia.

Joan departed from Beverly and made her way to Elizabeth's home. Elizabeth was having periods of restlessness and moaning as if in pain. Joan had examined her morphine pump and found it to be properly functioning. She noted the high level of medication infusing and wondered if something else was going on.

"What are we going to do now?" Georgia asked her.

"We're going to think about this for a little, on the front porch, come join me Ben," Joan said as she tapped the boy on his right arm, placed her arm around his shoulder and led him out of the house.

Once outside Joan asked Ben to take a walk with her to the store on the corner near his home. They walked slowly, Joan had picked a wild daisy and was pulling the pedals off one by one. Ben was chewing on a straw he had brought from the house. They said very little on the way, each with individual thoughts swimming in their heads. Joan went into the small community store first. She asked Ben what he wanted and he chose some candy and a Pepsi. Joan got a bottled water and the two walked leisurely back to the house and sat down on the concrete steps off the front porch.

Finally, when she had gathered her nerve, Joan spoke to Ben. "Ben you know your mama is dying right?" she asked him. He kept his eyes on the steps and shook his head yes. "Well," Joan continued, "Something is keeping your mama here. I think she is in a lot of pain. She's not having a good time here Ben. But I think she is afraid to let go for some reason. Maybe she is afraid to leave you."

The boy looked up at her with wide eyes, like a deer that had been spotlighted. Then Joan watched his eyes fill with tears. "But..." he searched for the way to say what he thought, "... when she dies I will be all alone. I won't have a mommie any more."

Joan kneeled before him and held him to her with his head on her shoulder. "Listen to me, I don't ever want you to forget this O.K.? You will always have a mommie. You won't be able to see her but she will always be your mommie. Don't ever forget that you are somebody important because someone in your life loved you more than anything in the whole world. Don't ever forget how important you are."

They sat for a while until the boy stopped crying. Then Joan took his small hand in hers. "Ben, I'm going to have to ask you to do something very hard. Probably one of the hardest things you will ever do. I want you to go in by your mama's bed and hold her hand like this and tell her that she doesn't have to worry about you. Tell her you will be all right and you are going to grow up strong, without drugs. Tell her you will miss her but you will see her again. Ask her to look down from heaven and check on you from time to time. Because you are going to try hard to make her proud of you. Do you think you can do that?"

The boy rubbed the tears away from his eyes and nodded his head and answered, "Yes."

76

"Good," Joan said. Joan told him "It will be the beginning of you growing up." After they were both better composed they went into Elizabeth's bedroom. Ben stood by the bed and did just as Joan had asked him to do. Then he kissed his mother's hand. Georgia took him by the hand and helped him get ready for a nap. Joan sponged Elizabeth's head and gave her more pain medicine. But Elizabeth made no gesture of recognition to her. She was in a deep peaceful sleep now. The kind of sleep one goes into when the angels are busy making final arrangements for departure.

That evening as Joan finished her calls she stopped by the roadside to pick one last bunch of daffodils for Elizabeth. She took them by and placed them on Elizabeth's pillow, close to her nose. "Fair thee well my friend," Joan whispered as she stood close by Elizabeth's bedside. "Sweet dreams and happy thoughts."

Four days later Mike, Laura and Joan attended the home going of Elizabeth at the Antioch Baptist Church. The church, although meek in appearance, was filled with spirit. The spirit of God, Elizabeth, and all of her family. It was like no other funeral Joan had ever attended.

Sweet songs of salvation rang from the choir, filling the building to the rafters with praise of the day and of Elizabeth's life. The theme of the program was that, "She's not troubled now, she's in the Lord's care."

When the choir led the congregation in, "Just a Closer Walk with Thee," no one was sitting, all hands were lifted in praise, and everyone swayed left to right in gentle rhythm. Amens and hallelujahs rang out. The minister started the eulogy in slow talk and ended with a song of his own, again guiding the entire church in praise.

Joan left the funeral, filled with renewed spirit, feeling like she could go on another day. She and Mike talked about it on the way home. "I've never been to anything like that. It was a celebration," she told him.

"Yeah I know, I've heard about funerals like that before, I've heard people talking and saying, 'she had a good funeral', now I know what they were talking about."

When Joan got home Brad asked, "How was the funeral?"

With enthusiasm in her voice she answered him. "I want

a black preacher and a black funeral when I die!"

"Mom," he reminded her, "You can't have a black preacher, you're Catholic remember? And you're not black."

"Well, here's what you do when I die. You find yourself a southern black priest and tell him to forget for a while that he's Catholic and remember that he's black and do my funeral with spirit." Joan responded, in her answer for everything way.

"All right Mom, all right," Brad said, shaking his head and smiling.

ELEVEN

Joan sat in the driveway a long time. Since she had not had lunch yet that day, she decided to sit there and watch something she had never seen before, if it took all of her half hour break. She was watching a full grown owl sitting on a low tree limb, watching her. One of her favorite things in the world was large birds of prey. And one of her favorite patients was Opal Rimes.

Joan knew she wasn't suppose to have favorites among her patients. Honestly, she loved them all. But she was bonded to Opal. She had cared for Opal for almost a year. Joan found the eighty eight year old grandmother interesting and entertaining.

Opal lived on a big farm in the country. Just the drive to her home was a pleasure. Through cornfields and tobacco fields and cotton fields, Joan would drive. Joan had commented once when she went there. "I've never seen cotton fields around here, I didn't know cotton grew around here."

To which Opal had replied, "Oh yes, I hated cotton fields when I was growing up. My daddy made me work in them all the time because it was something I was strong enough to do. I used to pick and pick for what seemed like hours. Then when I would sit down on the bag to take a break it would condense to about a third of it's size. I learned fast not to do that 'cause Daddy wouldn't let me quit until my bag was full. I never thought I'd see the day when I didn't have to pick cotton."

Opal's farm was very updated. She leased the fields out to neighboring farmers who farmed them in exchange for upkeep of the barns and fences.

Opal had a million stories and she loved to tell them to Joan. Since Joan's visits were long and Joan saved it until the end of the day, she felt like Joan was more interested in hearing them than anyone else she knew.

Joan used to tell her, 'I saved the best for last'. That made Opal's face light up. Opal loved her nurse like a grand daughter.

"Who lives in all those huge houses that are being built behind your farm, out on the lake?" Joan had asked Opal once.

Opal laughed and said, "Oh, doctors and such." Then she told Joan how when she and her husband were young they had the opportunity to buy as much lake front property as they wanted for five dollars an acre.

"Oh, Opal you didn't!" Joan remarked, dropping her jaw.

"Well, I told my husband I wasn't interested in that I had all the land I needed and that land would never amount to anything because nobody would ever want to live that far out."

"Oh Opal, if you had just bought fifty dollars of that land you would be a multi-millionaire now," Joan told her.

"Yeah, and then I could hire you for my private duty nurse. I'd build both of us a big house and you would just stay here and take care of me all the time."

"That would be lovely, my dear," Joan replied. And the two broke into a robust laugh.

One day as Joan examined Opal the two talked about gifts and talents. Joan commented on all of Opal's talents. Her green thumb and her cooking. Opal commented that her mother had the talent of 'use for'.

"What's that?" Joan asked her.

And through twinkling eyed recollection the older woman began her story. "You know, she would use for people who were sick."

Joan wasn't sure she understood. "Do you mean she would pray for them?"

"No, not exactly," Opal continued. "Like if someone was sick they would come here and she would say some things, and sometimes she would make a paste out of herbs and rub it on their affliction."

"What kind of things did she say?" Joan asked.

"Well, it would differ, according to what their problem was," Opal replied.

"How would she know what to say?" Joan asked her, she had stopped her examination at this point.

"She would look in that book she had and say whatever it told her to say." Opal was very matter of fact with her reply.

Joan pursed her lips and studied Opal for a few moments. Then she sheepishly grinned and asked, "So... your mother practiced witchcraft, hun?"

Opal laughed, "That's what some people called it anyway. The doctors used to get mad at her. They would tell people they had to go to the hospital and they would come here first and get her to use for them and see if it helped. Old Doctor Zeb would get mad and tell them that she was just an old witch and it wouldn't help them none. But once there was a baby in the hospital with fever and it had been there three days and hadn't began to get better. It's daddy brought it here and she used for it and rubbed a little salve in it's mouth and that baby was better the next day. Man Doc Zeb was mad. He came out here and told her that she risked that baby's life, that it could have died. But she told him that the baby's daddy came to her and that she didn't go seeking these people out."

"Wow!" Joan teased, "I never knew a real live daughter of a witch before." And the two ended another visit with a good laugh.

Opal was always busy doing something. Just after she was told she wouldn't live much longer Joan had a very difficult time finding her to do the visits. Opal, taking this hospice deal to heart, decided to spend as much time as she could doing all the things she had always wanted to do but never had the time. She ate at a different restaurant every night, and visited different shops near her home. She tired of this long before she died though, and decided she had enough to do 'down on the farm.'

Opal was such a joy to care for that it was easy for Joan to forget just how sick she was and that she was terminally ill. Due to Opal's facade, Joan had to constantly remind herself that Opal was a hospice patient. It took Joan a long time to learn to interpret Opal's unique language. Joan eventually learned the patterns which went along with Opal's vital signs.

Joan explained it in team conference once when it was Opal's time to be reviewed. "When she says, 'Oh, I'm just fine', it means she has only had to take pain medicine twice that day. When she says she's 'fair to middling', that means she has been able to do very little that day. And when she says 'Oh, not too bad', she's been in the bed for the last two days, taking pain medicine every three hours and she feels like someone beat her up and took her lunch money." Opal would sometimes have the bulletin from the House of Prayer on her skin somewhere, under her clothes. Joan knew Opal believed it helped with her pain. Another sign of pain that Opal had not reported to Joan.

Opal never ceased to be an inspiration to Joan. Her home was always neat as a pin and she was always kind, no matter how bad she felt. It was of great concern to Joan that she would have trouble handling herself when Opal died. It was the first time Joan had become this attached to a patient in hospice. Or, she was almost ashamed to admit, to anyone outside her family and small circle of friends. It wasn't fair, or professional, that she thought of the visits to Opal's home as her therapy. She was suppose to be the nurse in this relationship, not the one on whom blessings were bestowed. But Opal was alone much of the time, and even though she was surrounded by relatives, they were busy with their own lives. Opal looked forward to Joan's visits. She arose early on the days when Joan was coming and checked the window with every passing car, like a friend keeps watch out for another. Opal worried about Joan when the weather was bad. This concerned Joan too. She saw her role as bringing a little happiness to the patients, not to increase their worry. But neither made any effort to change things.

By the time Opal died she and Joan knew all about each other. They knew all each others families names and their histories. Opal knew about Joan's children, their names, birthdays, and dreams. Once Opal gave Joan some purple iris to plant in her yard. Joan planted them with care, selecting a prime bed and carefully tilling the soil. She was so upset when she went out the next day to find her iris all over her yard, some drug off into the woods by the family dog. Joan cringed when Opal asked her how her iris were doing. The two laughed when Joan told Opal about how she scolded the dog, as if he knew what she was talking about.

"Could you do me a favor before you go?" Opal asked Joan.

"Sure, anything for you," Joan obliged.

"Could you please thread my needle with black thread?" As Joan went into the sewing room to get Opal's sewing kit something caught her eye. It was a quilt, small, and yellowed with time. "Opal, what is this?" Joan asked her as she came back to the living room.

"That's a quilt I made years ago, in Miss Evans' class in the fourth grade."

"Oh, wow!" Joan was amazed at the artwork before her. The quilt was crude in workmanship, but wonderful just the same. It was hand sewn by children. It was worn and had to be handled with much care.

"Tell me about school," Joan asked Opal as she threaded the needle.

"Well, the thing I remembered most was that fourth grade year. Miss Evans was mean. And you know me, I would laugh when she got mad and she would get on to me. She would make me stand in the corner and I would end up laughing even harder, I just couldn't help it." Opal took a deep breath and her eyes twinkled as she remembered. She continued her story.

"Shut up!" she would yell at us. But her favorite pet was Elisa Morgan. Elisa was a straight A student and her best friend was Betty. Every time Miss Evans would get mad she would call Elisa or Betty to give the right answer and show us up.

"Once we were studying history and Miss Evans asked a question and asked for volunteers to answer. Well, none of us volunteered so she called on a few of us. When we failed to answer right she'd say, 'sit down, you're just stupid!'"

"So, then she called on Betty to answer the question. Betty stood up and turned her head and looked at us, you know, like she was so smart... and got the answer wrong too. Miss Evans told her to 'sit down!' Then she called on Elisa. 'Elisa, would you please tell this stupid class the answer to the question.' Poor Elisa didn't know what to do, she didn't have a clue what the answer was. 'Sit down, you're just as stupid as the rest of 'em!'" I just died laughing. I spent the rest of the day writing some line on the board over and over."

"What did you write, 'I will not laugh at stupid people?'" Joan asked her.

"Probably something like that," Opal replied.

Joan finished threading the needle and gave it to Opal. "Well, I have to go now, as much as I hate to." Joan hugged Opal and gathered her things and headed for home.

One sunny day the two walked arm in arm out by Opal's flower garden. Smelling gardenias and gazing at marigolds. Joan could see Opal getting weaker. "I have a suggestion for you." Joan told her. "I think you should write some of the things you know down for your grandchildren. It may not mean much to them now but it will in years to come. Your generation has so much you could tell us." Opal didn't seem to think much of the idea but she said she would consider it.

It was early fall when Joan got the call to come to Opal's home. Her daughter had found her. She was sitting in her chair with her glasses on her head. She had a notebook on her lap. She had been writing about her history. All the things she wanted her family to know. And all about her 'hospice angel' who came to check on her twice a week.

Joan had to leave work that day. She went to Price's pond and watched the mallards. She remembered all that Opal had taught her. She said a prayer for Opal and apologized for not being there. "I'm sorry that I wasn't there for you. But I know you weren't alone. I know the angels were with you," Joan said. She sat on the side of the pond for two hours and watched the changing shadows on the water, created by clouds that blocked the sunlight and then, like magic, let it shine through again. Even the mallards were quiet today, Joan noticed.

That night Joan could hardly sleep, but when she did she had a dream. She could see Opal walking down a wide white paved road. The road was surrounded by beautiful fields and woods with branches hanging low with green leaves, and flowers. Joan stood and called to Opal to come back. Opal turned to look at her once. She smiled the sweetest, most peaceful smile. But she didn't say anything. Joan said, "She's not coming back." Then Opal turned and began to walk on farther into the garden.

Joan got a call from Opal's daughter several weeks later.

84

She wanted Joan to have something from Opal's home. Something by which she could remember Opal. Joan told her she knew exactly what she wanted. "Could you please make a copy of the entry into her notebook where she wrote about me. I want that more than anything." Opal's daughter agreed and Joan received the copy in the mail a week later. She placed it in her Bible where she would see it and read it from time to time.

When you are weak I will be strong
When you are in pain I will be the comforter
When you are sleeping I will be silent
When you are crying I will be the shoulder for your head

When you are happy I will rejoice with you
When you are sad I will smile for you
When you are afraid I will pray with you
When you are ready I will let you go

For mine is a precious position
A labor of love
Our days together are few and
Each step you take I will take too

TWELVE

Andrew Christen settled into the leather recliner in one of Dr. Gray's therapy rooms. The room was tastefully decorated, but it was like going to the dentist. Nothing could disguise the reason he was there. He had just sat down in the blue chair, that even resembled a dentist chair, and put his feet up when the nurse came in and started his intravenous fluid. The needle didn't hurt much since he had a small port under his skin to receive it. It had been placed about a year ago because his veins had become so difficult for the nurses to access for blood drawing and giving his chemotherapy.

Andrew looked up at the poison in the bottle. He watched as it made it's way down the tubing and into his arm. Drip, drip, drip. The poison that was known as chemotherapy. He had tolerated it well at one time, five years ago when his cancer first appeared in his prostate. But it was different now. Dr. Gray had described this as a third line chemotherapy agent, whatever that meant, and told Andrew it was the strongest medicine he could give him. It was his last hope.

It seemed strange to Andrew that the medicine that was suppose to cure him made him so deathly ill. He watched how the nurses carefully handled the substance. How they took painstaking measures to avoid contact with it. How they never broke technique and always wore their gloves. Somehow seeing how they handled it so carefully made him question why he continued to absorb so much of this toxic substance into his body.

Somewhere after the first ten minutes Andrew drifted off

to sleep. He was awakened by the nurse, ever carefully, removing the needle from his arm. He sat up to roll down his sleeve and button his cuff. As he walked to the desk the receptionist got the appointment book to schedule Andrew's next treatment. "We need to see you again in three weeks," she was saying.

But Andrew interrupted her, "No Miss, I'm not going to be back in three weeks to take more treatment."

The receptionist looked at him and asked him to please wait, "I would like for you to have the opportunity to discuss this with Dr. Gray," she replied, nervously adjusting her glasses.

Andrew was shown to a private room where Dr. Gray soon joined him. "What's up Andrew?" The doctor asked.

"Well, I've been thinking about this a great deal lately. I feel lucky that you've helped me enjoy five good years since my surgery. But, I'm tired now. I come here and take treatment, then for a week after that I have to come here for a shot every day. Then I have to take blood, so I can come back and take more treatment. It's gotten to be a vicious cycle. I'm sick most of the time after a treatment. When I stop vomiting it's time to come back again. You've told me the last two times you checked my tumor markers that my cancer is growing rapidly, not stopping or slowing."

"If you stop treatment now you may not live long, you know that," Dr. Gray said.

Andrew nodded acknowledging his understanding of what the doctor was telling him. "I've always had a strong faith. And I've been thinking that by staying here, in this suspended animation state, I am denying myself the rewards of a better life that is waiting for me. It's time. Besides, it's like that movie where Clint Eastwood said 'dying ain't much of a living.'" They both chuckled, a forced nervous chuckle, and Dr. Gray had no choice but to support Andrew's decision.

Dr. Gray told Andrew, "I want to make a referral for you to hospice."

"Why?" Andrew asked, "What is hospice?"

"They care for people who have a life limiting illness, who decide not to pursue curative treatment. It's a very good organization. They will be of great help to you and your family," Dr. Gray explained.

Andrew agreed. "I'll probably need all the help I can get."

Dr. Gray called the next day and spoke with Faye. Faye, who had a good relationship with the doctors in town, told him she would send Joan McRae out to see Andrew the next day.

As Joan approached the front of Andrew's country home she saw him, standing on the deck enjoying the cool morning air. He was tastefully dressed in a blue denim shirt and dockers, and was sipping coffee. Andrew was a tall, about six two, handsome man of fifty, with hazel eyes. He had a kind demeanor and the perfection of his chemotherapy induced bald head made him look almost angelic.

Joan joined him and introduced herself. "Welcome, come on in." Andrew invited her through the deck gate. When he spoke his voice was raspy from weakness created by cancer and chemotherapy. Joan noticed the skin of his hands had purple spots and was so thin it looked like light blue parchment paper.

Andrew's golden retriever joined the two and sniffed the stranger. Joan petted him and Andrew tried to shoo the dog away. "It's all right, he's not bothering me, I'm used to it." Joan said as she petted the large dog. "You have a beautiful home, it seems very peaceful here," Joan told Andrew. She turned and followed his gaze out over the land that spread out before them. "How much of this land is yours?"

Andrew was always happy to talk about his farm. He had been raised there and his sons would soon be keeping the farm running. "You see the top of those trees over there where the paint factory is?"

Joan nodded.

"We own down to there on both sides of the road, as far as you can see either way, about two hundred acres all together."

Joan was impressed to see such a beautiful piece of land. "It is becoming almost unheard of in this county at this time, what with all the rapid growth replacing such large parcels of farmland with developments and strip malls."

"Come, let me show you something," Andrew led Joan down the deck steps to a half acre garden spot. The garden had been plowed and Andrew had planted it with corn. He told Joan "I know this will be my last garden, but I wanted to enjoy planting season one last time." As the two turned and walked back toward the house Joan caught a heavy smell of honeysuckle that grew on the banks of a stream running through Andrew's land. She laid her head back and breathed in the sweet smell.

As they neared the house they walked through a garden trellis covered with an ivy with small white, sweet smelling, flowers. Andrew told her it was Carolina Jasmine. He explained, "It is still called Confederate Jasmine in some states. We have a grandchild due in September, it is a girl, our daughter's first. They plan to name her Jasmine."

"How wonderful for you all," Joan replied. The two went into the house and Joan began introducing Andrew to hospice. Mary Christen, Andrew's wife of thirty one years, joined them. She sat on the couch arm beside Andrew and placed her arm around his shoulders. Andrew introduced her to Joan.

Andrew and Mary had many questions for Joan, who spent two hours answering them. They asked her everything from what hospice could do for them to when she thought Andrew would die. Joan assured them, "I don't know when he will die. I prefer to help you focus on living one day at a time, and enjoying each day for what it has to offer you. We can prepare for your dying, but you are still living now and we will spend most of our time controlling symptoms you will have, and concentrating on making each day the best it can be for you."

"Well all I ask is just don't let him hurt," Mary told Joan.

"I'll do my best," Joan promised. Joan finished her paperwork and left after making an appointment to see Andrew in two days.

That night the moon was bright. It shone through the window of Mary and Andrew's bedroom. Mary could see the stars shining as she laid close to Andrew, enveloped in his embrace. He was sleeping. She laid her left hand on his chest. She could feel the beating of his heart and she could hear the breathing of his lungs. She listened carefully to each sound he made. What would it be like when she laid her hand on his chest and felt nothing, she wondered.

Mary tried hard to be as positive as possible when Andrew was awake. She didn't want to waste one minute with him. There would be time enough later for her tears. Besides, she felt, if she started crying now she may never stop.

Andrew and Mary spent their days doing all the things they wanted to do. Since the treatments had stopped, Andrew had more energy and felt better. He knew it would be temporary but he was determined to make the most of it while it lasted. Joan had worked with Dr. Gray to get Andrew on a stronger time released pain and nausea medicine so he could be more active. Every day he spent a couple of hours in his garden, weeding, watering, looking at his plants. Afterwards he would sleep for hours.

Laura had visited and helped the couple with final funeral arrangements. She noticed Mary's eyes swell with tears as she signed her name to the papers.

Mary watched Andrew closely. They sat on the deck one Friday evening in a rocking bench, softly swaying back and forth. Mary looked over the coffee cup clasped in her hands. She was pretending to blow the coffee, but Andrew was keenly aware of her intense stare. "What are you doing?" Andrew asked her.

Mary blushed, she was embarrassed about being caught. "I'm trying to take all of you into my memory. I don't want to forget one thing about you, I want to remember this moment for the rest of my life. This night, every smell, every sound, everything."

Andrew moved close to her and softly said, "Then don't ever forget how much I love you, and don't ever forget this," and he pulled her close and kissed her. It was a long, passionate kiss, one Mary Christen would never forget. She blushed again as she took his hand and led him up to their bedroom.

By the time Andrew's corn was knee high he was becoming weaker. Two months had passed since his hospice admission. It was now early July. Joan had called Dr. Gray several times to increase his medicine. He was started on oxygen, and he was having trouble walking without getting short of breath. Mary rearranged their bedroom so Andrew could sit by the large window and see his garden. Every morning the couple would sit by the window and have breakfast and talk about how the garden was progressing and of the coming harvest. Mostly Mary would listen and Andrew would 'direct'.

It was on one such morning when Mary had her breakdown. "When that garden is harvested and Jasmine is born my life will be complete," Andrew said. And Mary could no longer hold back her emotions. She cried for hours. Deep sobbing tears at first, from deep within her inner soul. Her heart had threatened to break for months and had finally succeeded. Andrew held her close the whole day.

She told him, "I am so afraid to be alone. I don't want to live without you."

Andrew just let her talk and held her. The two spent the whole day in their room together. In a way it was the best day they had spent together for a long time. It was the first time in a long while that Mary had let him know exactly how she felt. Andrew had always been the strong one. Mary, filled with self doubts, wondered how she would take on that role now?

He held her in his arms and assured her that she would do fine and he would be there to help even though she couldn't see him.

Mary finally drifted off to sleep early in the night. Andrew got up and sat in the chair by the window. He found some paper and a pen and wrote a letter to his family. He told how proud he was of each of them, and about how wonderful his life was and how lucky he was to have been chosen to live thirty one years with his beautiful bride, Mary. Andrew asked them to take good care of each other. And he asked them to tell Jasmine all about him.

When that was done he folded the letter and placed it in his sock drawer where Mary would find it later. Then he slipped under the covers, snuggled in close to Mary, and fell fast asleep.

Joan came to see Andrew three times a week by the time his corn was full grown. He was getting weaker and she was trying to stay ahead of his symptoms. About once a week Mary asked her, "How much longer?" Mary confessed she was concerned. "Jasmine isn't due for another month and Andrew is so very weak."

Joan told her that, "Sometimes people can will themselves to make it until an event comes to pass. Don't give up hope yet. If he wants to live to see that baby, he may do it."

Mary told Joan there had been a change in Andrew, one that she hadn't expected. "He seems afraid now, where he hadn't been before."

"Yeah," Joan told her, "It's normal to be afraid. We're human, we're afraid of the unknown. That doesn't mean he has lost his faith. Death is like going someplace where you've never been before, and you don't know what it's going to be like there or how to prepare for the trip. Has he started talking to people who have gone before him?"

"Yes, he will seem to be staring into space and talking to people that I can't see," Mary answered.

Joan continued to question Mary, "Have you seen changes in the dog?"

Mary looked concerned, "Why, yes I have. I can't for the life of me get him to eat or drink, and he doesn't want to leave the room. He just keeps staring at Andrew and whines and looks up. What do these things mean?"

Joan thought carefully before she answered. "Some of us who are Christian believe these are angel experiences. Usually once these start death comes within a few weeks and the dying turn into themselves, detach from their surroundings and become ready to die. He may ask you if it's okay if he goes. If he does just tell him yes and that you will all be fine and will take care of each other. That usually brings about a peacefulness. Then it's easier for them to give up the struggle to stay alive and go on to a better life that awaits them."

Mary was very quiet and deep in thought about what Joan had told her. Joan went to the bedroom to see Andrew. He was sitting on the side of his bed. Joan sat down beside him and took his right hand, enveloping it in hers. She asked him, "Do you have any questions for me?"

He just nodded his head and said very little.

Joan asked him, "Are you at peace with your maker?"

He shook his head indicating that he was. "I'm going home soon Joan," was all he said.

"I know you are. And I trust you are ready. You are a good person Andrew, you are close to God. I feel sure you have nothing to fear. Is there anything else I can do for you, Andrew?" she asked him.

He only shook his head 'no' and smiled.

"Are you afraid Andrew?" He didn't answer. "You know it's okay if you are, but you won't be alone. Death is just part of life. And I believe that you will close your eyes to this life and awaken to your new life, in a better place." Joan hugged him.

And he responded. "Thank you," in a muffled tone.

Joan turned and looked out the windows. Andrew's sons were in the corn field, working. Joan could see ears of corn coming on quick but the plants weren't tasseled out yet and the ears were not fully grown. I wonder how long it takes for corn to tassel out? Joan thought. "Please don't be born late Jasmine," Joan whispered to herself as she looked over the green field of corn, and then back at Andrew.

One week later Joan was called to come and check on Andrew. Mary was having a difficult time arousing him. He seemed to be in a great deal of pain. Joan took his vital signs and explained to Mary what had to be done. The two worked to get his high fever down. Once that was done Andrew seemed more comfortable. He wasn't eating anything, and was drinking very little. Joan called Dr. Gray and got new medication orders.

She worked until she got his pain controlled. It seemed to take forever. When several hours had passed Joan and Mary were exhausted, but Andrew was comfortable, awake and talking to them.

Mary managed to get a cup of chicken soup in him before he drifted back off to sleep. Joan called his oldest son Michael to come and stay with Mary that night. "I don't think it's a good idea for them to be alone," Joan told Michael.

He agreed and said he "would be over shortly."

Joan crawled into her bed late, exhausted, but thankful. Laying on her pillow she suddenly remembered that she had forgotten to look at the corn. She made a mental note to do that the next morning.

Joan went by Andrew's house first on her route the next morning. She was somewhat surprised to see him dressed and having coffee in a wheelchair on the back porch. Michael had gotten him up and was preparing a makeshift ramp. He was going to take Andrew out to the cornfield to check the corn. Andrew wanted to see if it was ready for harvest.

"Ready to go Pop?" Michael asked as he came up the ramp, testing it's load handling capability.

Andrew handed his coffee cup to Mary and smiled. "I

94

sure am." And Joan and Mary watched as they made their way across the dew kissed morning grass to the garden. Andrew stood briefly to pick an ear of corn. He sat and peeled off the long green leaves covering the golden ear. When he had finally cleaned the corn of it's covering he took a bite of it. And Mary and Joan smiled as Andrew grinned and said, "It's ready."

The next two days Andrew pushed himself to the limits of exhaustion as he watched from his bedroom while his sons harvested the corn from the field. Andrew repeatedly told Mary that he was proud of the abundant harvest he had brought forth from his last garden on earth. But it was unclear to her if he were referring to the corn or his family.

The phone rang at Joan's house at seven o'clock the following day. Rae was calling to give her the news. Mary had called Rae, who was the nurse on call. "It's a girl! Jasmine arrived at three this morning. Seven pounds even, and twenty inches long." Joan heard Rae's words.

"She made it, Thank God!" Rae heard Joan reply. Joan called to congratulate Mary and Andrew and to tell them she would see them the next day.

Joan arrived at Andrew's home shortly after two in the afternoon on Friday. She noticed the silver Honda in the drive with an infant restraint seat in the rear. She walked into Andrew's bedroom as Elise laid Jasmine in the bed beside Andrew. The baby girl looked like an angel laying there with black hair and a white dress. Andrew leaned up on one elbow and gingerly touched the baby girl. "Oh, she's the most beautiful thing I've ever seen." Then leaning over he kissed the baby on her forehead.

Elise took pictures with a camera. Mary took one with her heart. Joan drank in the moment. It was almost too much for her and she left the room to wash her hands.

Joan just asked Andrew and Mary if they needed anything from her that day. They both said "no" so she left them to enjoy their family. She could check Andrew another day, today was too precious for questions and probes about cancer and pain. Days like this were few for Andrew and Mary.

Joan saw Andrew on Monday. He had spent much of his weekend with Elise and Jasmine who had moved in for the weekend. They had left shortly after Joan arrived. When she went to see Andrew Joan noticed rapid changes in his condition. His color was different and his blood pressure had dropped. His heart rate was rapid and bounding. He was trying to sleep but was in a great deal of pain, and having trouble breathing. "What do you think Joan?" Mary asked the nurse.

Joan looked into her eyes and replied, "Mary, I think Andrew is dying."

Mary started crying and nodded her head and said she knew it.

"I've done all I can with the medicine I have here. I'm going to make arrangements for some sort of intravenous or intradermal morphine to give him. I don't want him to struggle. I'll be back after I talk to Dr. Gray and I'll have everything I need with me when I come," Joan informed Mary.

Mary agreed and told Joan, "I'm going to call the children in the meantime."

Two hours later Joan was standing by Andrew's bedside. She was letting liquid morphine flow into a tubing which she was going to hook up to Andrew's skin to give him a slow continuous infusion of medication to keep him comfortable. His family were all there, softly talking and rubbing his head and holding his hand.

Leaning down Mary told him, "it's okay to go now. I know you are tired." Andrew looked up at the package as Joan prepared the pain relieving medication. Then he watched the medication make it's way down the tubing as it was prepared to go into his arm. Drip, drip, drip, as it filled the line. He smiled at his family and drifted off to sleep.

THIRTEEN

Lillian Edwards was at the end of the driveway when Joan came down the highway looking at each mailbox for the right house number. She spotted Lillian before she saw the numbers on the box. It was a cold morning and Lillian had on no coat or sweater. She seemed to be lost, looking in the mailbox for mail at nine o'clock in the morning. Joan soon saw Jeff Edwards, an apron tide around his waist, hurrying to the mailbox to direct Lillian away from the highway. His face was aged with stress, and a look of sheer terror adorned it. Then Joan saw the number on the mailbox. She turned into the drive and parked.

Jeff took Lillian by the hand and led her back inside. Joan got out of the car and followed the couple into their home. It was a beautiful place. It was small with two bedrooms, a cozy den, a roomy kitchen with windows on two sides so lots of sun shone in. There were two bathrooms, a formal living room, and a full basement. The house was not new, in fact Jeff and Lillian had raised two children to adulthood while living in it. But it had been excellently maintained and their son had updated the house over the years.

Jeff introduced himself and Lillian to Joan and sat down on a stool in front of Lillian, who had retired into her favorite recliner. Jeff was scolding Lillian for going to the highway. He was warning her about the danger and that if she kept doing things like that he would have to take her back to "the home."

Jeff started informing Joan about Lillian's mental state, as if he had to quickly explain his actions. "Lillian was diagnosed with Alzheimer's Disease six years ago, when she was sixty eight years old. She took the diagnosis hard, crying a lot. She made me promise not to let her live in an indignant way. I've done my best to keep that promise. When caring for her had started to become too much for us I searched all over the state of North Carolina for a nursing home which specialized in Alzheimer's Care. I found a good one in Morganton, on a beautiful mountain side with a breath taking panoramic view. It looked more like a resort than a nursing home. However, Lillian was unable to adjust to the home. She cried and begged us to take her home any time we came to see her. She constantly tried to leave the unit."

"The staff called me in for a meeting one day. The doctor wanted to start Lillian on antidepressant medication so she could deal better with her placement but I guess I had a different opinion. I showed up at the meeting with boxes and suitcases, thanked the staff for their interest and told them I had come to take Lillian home. The director of nursing met with me and offered her assistance in any way possible. I just wanted Lillian to be as happy as she possibly could. Seeing her in such distress was harder than the physical stress of caring for her myself," he sat still staring at Lillian as he told the nurse the story.

Jeff hoped that bringing Lillian home would settle her down, but Lillian had changed. Her memory and behaviors were worse now than when he had taken her to the nursing home. In desperation Jeff took Lillian to her doctor to have her medication adjusted and to find hope. His search led him to Doctor Withers, in their home town.

Doctor Withers was a young man, he had graduated from Duke University within the last year. "How are you today Lillian?" he asked as she and Jeff entered his office. Taking her hand in his he gently led her into the room, shook Jeff's hand and gazed into her eyes.

"How's your grandpa?" Jeff asked him.

"He's getting along okay. I was over there yesterday, and he was out trimming his apple trees, so I guess he can't complain." The two men smiled.

"And your grandma?" Jeff asked him.

"Oh, she's wonderful as always, and how's Miss Lillian today?" Dave Withers answered, directing the attention back to

Lillian.

After examining Lillian and questioning Jeff about her behavior he told them that it did not look good. He felt that Lillian had changed her level of dementia and would soon be entering the final stages of her disease. Dr. Withers advised Jeff to get some in home help and made a referral to hospice.

Sitting on the stool now Jeff could see that Lillian was more interested in the stranger that had come into her home than anything he was trying to tell her. Lillian smiled at Jeff and turned her eyes to Joan. She looked Joan up and down. Jeff shook his head in frustration. He was unable to figure out if Lillian had understood anything he had told her about the danger she had put herself in by going so close to the road.

Joan sat down close to Lillian and introduced herself. "Hi Lillian, my name is Joan McRae. I'm a nurse. Dr. Withers asked me to come and check on you for him." Lillian was good at pretending she understood everything that was going on. She was also, Joan sensed, suspicious of her being in their house.

Joan represented that something in her environment had changed. Change was very hard for Lillian. She looked at Joan through squinted eyes, as if she wasn't sure if she should know Joan or not. Joan kept assuring her that she was only there because Dr. Withers wanted her to help him keep a good check on her.

"Are you here to check my blood pressure? The doctor likes to watch my blood pressure," Lillian asked Joan.

Joan said, "Yes," hoping that thought would help Lillian accept her presence in the home.

Getting a true hold on what was actually going on in the home was a time consuming duty for Joan. The family had been through so much by the time they got help that it was difficult untangling their stories. By the time Joan had been at Lillian and Jeff's home for three hours she had learned enough of their history to get a good start on getting them the help they needed.

"There will be a meeting of the local chapter of The Alzheimer's Association in town next Monday. Jeff, do you think that you could attend that?" Joan was asking him.

Jeff stated, "Well, I don't know if I can make it. Lillian is difficult for other people to be with, and I have so much to do."

"Jeff have you ever been to one of these meetings, or called to take advantage of anything the community has to offer you in the way of help?" Joan asked.

"No, I didn't figure they could help me much and I haven't discussed Lillian with many people in town," Jeff admitted.

"I'm going to call The Alzheimer's Association and order the literature packet they give to new members. They have a lot to offer you Jeff. In the way of literature and support. I would appreciate it if you would try to attend just one of their meetings. I'll be sure Lillian has a volunteer from hospice here that evening so you won't have to worry about her." Jeff finally agreed to attend and give it one try. With that accomplished Joan set out to the office to work on a plan of care for Lillian.

Back at the office the nurses were busy doing their paperwork and talking. Joking with each other as usual. Somehow they got to talking about death and dying and what they could tell patients actually would happen. When Rae spoke up, "Well, I know what happens because I've been there."

Joan leaned back in her chair and rolled her eyes at Rae. "What do you mean you've been there?"

Rae explained. "A few years ago when I had a car wreck I was out and I got the strangest feeling. I was so peaceful and I was walking on the softest ground cover of thinly crushed sea shells and the air all around me was calm. I wasn't afraid because I knew where I was. I walked through a beautiful garden and then I came to these beautiful golden gates adorned with pearl. I wanted so badly to go in but then all of a sudden I was back in the emergency room and they were waking me up. I told them no, to please put me back under because I knew that if they would I could try to go back, but they would have no part of it. But I know why I went there."

"Why?" Joan asked her.

To which Rae replied, "Because I'm God's favorite." Rae, Joan and Beverly laughed out loud.

Joan turned to Beverly and teasingly mocked Rae. "First she was her mother's favorite, then she was Faye's favorite, now she's God's chosen one." They all laughed. After that Joan called Rae 'the chosen one' or 'fair hair child' whenever she saw her.

Joan met with Laura and Jennifer, who was in charge of

the hospice volunteers. She asked them to set up meetings with Jeff and his two children. Joan called Jeff and made arrangements for their next meeting.

Later that week when she made her visit, Joan slowed down as she neared the Edwards' house. She was scanning the area for Lillian. She was relieved when she saw Lillian and Jeff on their knees in front of the flower garden. Lillian had on her straw sun hat, and Jeff a baseball cap. Jeff was talking to her, telling her what each flower and plant was. Although she had once been quite an avid gardener, Lillian didn't remember any of the names of the plants in her garden. Jeff had lovingly tended the garden because it had meant so much to Lillian when she was healthy. It was the thing she had poured herself into when the children had grown up and moved out. Jeff told Joan that each time a child left the garden got bigger.

Lillian had won several blue and red ribbons from the county fair for her roses. They were her pride. Now, Jeff occasionally caught a glimpse of what he liked to think was realization in her eyes. But of course he could never be sure. But he just kept on trying, telling her the plants names and asking her to tell him the colors. She could remember some of them, but she mostly agreed with Jeff when he said to her, "Isn't that a pretty red or a bright yellow?"

Joan had gotten out of the Suburban and sat on the grass close to them where she could talk to Jeff. They discussed ways he could make the house and grounds more safe for Lillian. Jeff asked her to, "Make a list and I'll see about doing some of them. But I'll tell you we need to invest in a ramp right away. Lillian is fine going down steps but coming back up them is difficult for her and she often simply refuses to go. I spend almost half an hour some days just getting her into the house. Besides I don't want her not to be able to go outside if she can't walk."

During the visit a silver Jeep pulled up and a handsome, rugged outdoor type, man got out. He came over to the others and Jeff introduced him to Joan. He was Lillian's youngest child, her son David. David had wanted to meet Joan, he had some questions for her and invited her into the house. Joan could sense his reluctance to talk in front of his parents so she agreed, excusing herself from Jeff and Lillian.

Once inside David got himself a coke from the refrigerator and got one for Joan too. He didn't ask her if she wanted it, just poured it into a glass and sat it in front of her on the table. He was cordial but Joan could sense that he was getting his nerve up to say something difficult to her. The suspense was killing her, but she let him take his own good time. Finally it came.

"Look, I'm glad you're here for my dad. He needed help here years ago but he wouldn't get it. He has lived in a dream world where Lillian is concerned."

This left the door open for Joan to walk in. "And where are you in all of this David? What is your relationship with your parents like?"

He took a deep breath and chose his words carefully. "I help dad where I can. I keep the house repaired and the yard mowed. My sister runs errands and we stay with her when we need to."

Joan could hear a "but," coming from a mile away. David did not fail to disappoint her.

"But," there it was, "I lost my mother years ago. The woman who so lovingly raised me is gone from me, forever lost. What I see now, when I look at Lillian is the shell of a woman that used to be. That shell houses her heart, lungs, and other body parts, but her spirit, the part that made her my mom, the very essence of her soul is gone. That's not my mother out there in that garden. I'm telling you this because I want you to understand when I don't cry at the funeral. I've buried my mother piece by piece for six years now."

Joan was speechless. She really didn't know what to say to David. She just bowed her head and said, "That's a shame." She couldn't wait to get out of their home and to a telephone. She needed help from Laura or Mike, "NOW." Somehow she managed to return to the yard where Lillian and Jeff were just getting up from their garden spot. She finished her visit and got back into the Suburban and set out to find a place where she could collect her thoughts and to call the office.

All she could think was how much David was hurting. He must have so much guilt about something, she thought. She saw something when she had looked at him. He was in pain, she knew that. Joan recognized it because she had seen it before at the nursing home, on the Alzheimer's unit. Children who refused to visit their parents, because 'that's not my mom'. "What a cop out," she said out loud. "Even when life deals you a bad hand you're not suppose to turn your back on those you love and who love you."

When she got Laura on the phone Joan asked her if it was the disease that he was angry with or was he angry with Lillian, for leaving him?

Of course Laura didn't know yet. "Sounds like I've got a lot of work to do with this family."

"Good luck!" Joan retorted.

Lillian was able to walk, and that meant every time Joan visited her she could be found outside. It was her favorite place. Joan spent a lot of her time over the next several weeks helping Jeff make the home safer for her. He put child safety locks on all cabinets and put all medications and cleansers away. He built a pretty white picket fence around the front yard. He planted roses along it hoping Lillian would be so interested in them she wouldn't pay the fence much attention.

Jeff had attended and enjoyed the meeting of The Alzheimer's Association. He told Joan all about the people he met. There was a woman there who was caring for her husband. Jeff was able to ask her lots of questions. Everything from ironing to cooking. The two hit it off from the start.

Jeff listened with great interest to what the others had been through. "I can't believe there are other people in the community going through the same thing I am," he told Joan with an air of great relief. "I can't believe this has been here for me all along, and all I had to do was reach out for the support before." He attended the meetings on a regular basis after that. And soon he was asking the children to stay with Lillian so he could join a small group of these new friends for dinner once a month.

One bright Tuesday morning Lillian and Joan sat in chairs on the front lawn. While Joan checked Lillian over a lady mail carrier came walking toward them to deliver a package. "Good morning!" the mail carrier said in her sing-song voice.

"Good morning." Lillian smiled and nodded.

As the mail carrier turned and walked away Lillian waved and under her breath said, "Bitch." Joan recognized this to be characteristic of Alzheimer's stricken persons.

Joan's mouth dropped open. "Lillian... did you say what I think you said?" Joan teased her.

Lillian laughed and said, "Yes I did." And then the moment passed as fast as it came.

Laura met with David and with Jeff. At team conference, when the team discussed Lillian's case, Laura talked the most. "David is angry with his mother for being sick and how that has affected their family. He feels that their family was once the happiest he knew. He has been raised with much love and care. As Lillian's disease has gotten worse she has forgotten him, and he feels abandoned. His anger toward the disease had been transferred to his mother. He failed to see that it was the disease he was angry with and not Lillian."

"As we worked with David, and explained his reactions to him, he opened up to me. He seemed relieved to hear what I told him. He had been angry with himself because he felt so bad about the way he reacted to his mother. He didn't know how to handle all his feelings. David cried for a solid hour when he realized that I knew what he had hid from everyone for so long. As he understood more of what was going on with him he started spending more time with Lillian, not just around the house, avoiding her. Lillian is enjoying her time with him. David was finally able to forgive himself for the way he had acted all these years."

"As the two sat together on the couch one day looking at pictures of David's twin sons Lillian looked at him and said, 'I think I used to know you, did I used to be your mother?'"

"David was able to kiss Lillian on the cheek softly and say, 'You are still my mother, you'll always be my mother.'"

"Lillian smiled at the handsome stranger son sitting by her side and said nothing else."

"Jeff is adjusting well to having help. He has begun to talk about his life after Lillian's death, something he had not previously even thought about. I've encouraged him, telling him that it was not only normal but healthy. I assured him that he was in no way being disrespectful to Lillian." Soon after Laura talked with Jeff he made Lillian's funeral arrangements.

There was a chill running down Joan's spine as she listened to Laura talk that morning. She tried hard not to cry, but she was one of the few who had managed not to. And before the conference was over, she, like all the others had to have the Kleenex passed her way. She turned to Faye and said, "I love a good love story don't you?"

And wiping her eyes and smiling Faye agreed.

Once Lillian began to decline things happened quickly. She became uninterested in getting out of bed one Saturday in early May. Within a week she didn't get up at all. The next week she stopped eating. She died peacefully on Mother's Day with Jeff, David, her daughter, and Joan by her bedside.

David was able to support Jeff through this trying time in his life. Jeff was able to go on with his life. He began dating Rosemary from the Alzheimer's Association. Her husband had died just before Lillian. The two were married in a simple ceremony one year later. David served as the best man.

FOURTEEN

Joan stood in disbelief as her mother told her the news. "Your Aunt Sue had some severe head pain so she went in to have a catheterization... and the doctors found a blockage in the artery on the right side of her neck. They went in to try and remove it... and it broke lose and went to the base of her brain. She's in room 7286 if you want to see her."

"This cannot be happening," Joan thought.

"I'll keep you posted of any changes," Joan heard her mother say.

"All right, thank you," Joan said and made plans to see her aunt over the weekend.

The next evening she felt more re-assured. Patricia called to tell her that her aunt had opened her eyes, talked to her family, and even smiled at one of their jokes. Joan felt relieved in her decision that she could wait until the weekend to go check on Sue.

After church on Sunday she drove the forty miles to see her aunt, hoping for good news. She entered the hospital and took the elevator to the seventh floor. The hospital was old and in bad need of renovation. It was a large institution but all the money in the county went to support the nearby teaching hospital, at the university. Joan got off the elevator and walked down the hall to Sue's room.

Joan braced herself as she entered the room. It was a good thing she did. Otherwise she would have went ballistic when she saw what 'they' had done to her aunt. As she saw the bottle of milk colored feeding hanging from a chrome pole she knew what had happened. She quickly looked to see that there was no feeding tube in Sue's nose. She lifted the covers and checked. As suspected, the feeding tube had been surgically placed in Sue's stomach.

Joan replaced the cover and touched Sue's hand. No response. She rubbed her face and spoke to her, "Aunt Sue," she said, hopeful. "Aunt Sue, hey, ... can you speak to me?" she sighed, less hopeful. She rubbed her aunt's back, then her arm, "Oh, Aunt Sue I'm here, I want you to know I'm here," she stated, all hope vanishing from her words.

Joan knew that day that hope was slim for a full recovery, if Sue lived at all. She looked for any sign of hope in her aunt's condition. The vital signs were unstable. There were signs of heart failure. Sue opened her eyes only once that day, Joan was standing by her side and hoped against hope that Sue saw her and knew it was her, that she had not forsaken her at this time.

Joan eventually turned her attention to the others present in the room. She found the nurse's notes from the last few days. Each day Sue had shown signs of decline. She was on multiple medications. Her doctors had hoped to stabilize her but were now talking to her family about transferring her to a nursing home after discharge from the hospital, if she lived to be discharged. "Over my dead body," Joan thought. She knew that Sue had hoped she would never have to go to a nursing home.

Sue had watched her beloved sister lose her spirit, her will to live, and all but lose her sanity in a nursing home a few years ago. Her sister had gone from a stout one hundred sixty pounds to ninety eight pounds. She cried all the time. It had been heartbreaking for Sue, and for Joan. But neither one of them had any power to change the decision. Sue made the statement when she read Mae's obituary that it should have cited a broken heart as the cause of death. Joan promised Sue she would not have to go to a nursing home.

Joan found her aunt's brother. "Arthur, what have they told you about this feeding tube, and her condition?" she asked him.

"They just said she had to have it because she wasn't eating," he answered. Just as Joan thought, he knew very little. He was exhausted. He was tired from traveling from out of state to see his sister, and all the decisions he and his wife had been asked to make. "You know you did have a choice in this decision, right?" Joan asked Arthur. "You also don't have to send her to a nursing home," Joan continued.

"What type of choices do we have?" they both wanted to know.

Joan began to fill them in on the part the hospital staff had left out. "You can take her home, she doesn't have to go to a nursing home. And you can stop this tube feeding any time. If she isn't going to get better, why do we want to prolong her in this state so she can decline, and be miserable?"

"Who will take care of her if she doesn't go to a nursing home?" Arthur was speaking this time.

"If she shows no sign of improvement and the doctors tell you she won't get better, tell them you want this tube removed and they can make arrangements to send her home by ambulance. I will take a leave of absence from work and take care of her, in her bed, in her home, with her dog by her side. She will live a shorter time but she may be able to know she is home with her friends and family by her side."

On the way home Joan discussed Sue's condition with her mom.

"Well, what do you think?" Patricia was asking.

Joan explained to her mother what she had seen in the nurses words. Those words drew a picture of Sue declining with each passing day. She explained that unless this stopped, Sue would not live long. But Joan didn't want her to die in the hospital. Joan spent most of the rest of the day in silent prayer vigil for Sue.

That night Joan told James, "I can't bear the thought of Sue lingering on and on in a suspended half life. If Sue leaves the hospital I want to take her home and care for her there or bring her to our home."

"Okay," James agreed without hesitation.

After two weeks had passed, Sue was no better and no worse. The hospital discharge planner had talked to Arthur and told him Dr. Gray had requested arrangements be made to transfer Sue to a nursing home. Spring Gardens, a beautiful long term care facility near Sue's home had an open bed for her.

Arthur was on the phone with Joan. His words were choking with tears and exhaustion. "I don't know what to do."

Joan told him, "I'll be there within the hour you go have something cold to drink and try to relax until I get there."

When Joan arrived at the hospital she went to the nurses station and asked where she might find Ms. Raymond, the discharge planner. The nurses agreed to page Ms. Raymond.

"Have her come up here please," Joan requested. The tone of her voice and the look on her face must have relayed the seriousness in her request, because the nurses did not offer any excuses. "I'll be in my aunt's room, I will expect to see Ms. Raymond shortly," Joan said and turned. She walked swiftly down the corridor to find Arthur.

Marie Raymond entered Sue's room to find Arthur and Joan talking quietly by the window. Joan turned and crossed the room offering her hand first to the tall, young, blond, discharge planner. "I hear you need to see me and that it's urgent. What may I do to help you?" Marie offered.

Joan was very matter of fact, and got directly to the point. "While I understand Spring Gardens is a beautiful and well respected home it's not my aunt's home. My aunt specifically stated she never wanted to go to a nursing home. My family is very appreciative of all that the staff and doctors here have done for her, and for us, but we will be taking her home. On Monday have her discharged and taken by ambulance to her home. Call hospice and have them admit her on Tuesday. I will be assuming responsibility for her care. Oh… and one more thing, you can arrange to have the tube feedings stopped, but leave the tube in… in case we need it for medications. I will need a DNR form from Dr. Gray. We will take it with us."

Joan didn't leave much time for questions and Marie knew she meant business. Marie turned to Arthur and asked, "Are you in agreement with all of these requests?"

He nodded his head yes, and stated, "I think it is the best thing for my sister." Once back home, Joan called Faye and arranged to take a family leave of absence to care for Sue. She kissed her family good-bye and they all promised to help each other until she returned.

Sue arrived home on Tuesday, around eleven in the morning. Joan, Arthur and Cocoa were there to welcome her home. Joan had prepared her room with fresh cut flowers, her favorite pillow and blanket, and soft music, the big band era kind that Sue had always loved. And although she didn't respond, Joan talked to her. "It will be all right now, you're home, in your own room, and Cocoa is right here." Joan lifted the small terrier onto the bed, where he snuggled close to Sue and settled for a long nap.

Joan walked out onto the screened porch attached to the end of the house. She could see a car pulling up the long drive. Her mother had arrived at Sue's home. The two agreed to stay and help each other get through this. "How long do you think this will take?" Patricia asked.

"Because Sue is well hydrated I think we are looking at eight or nine days, maybe two weeks," Joan answered.

Her mother sighed and told Joan, "I'm glad that you are here to take care of things. I'll help all I can but you may have to tell me what to do."

"Don't worry, I'm good at that," Joan responded. The two laughed and Patricia walked in to check on Sue.

Joan busied herself with Sue's needs much of the time. She noticed how slowly the hands on the clock turned. Funny how when she was only the nurse the hands seemed to fly around the clock face, she thought. But being there, in Sue's house, as the family, time slowed to a crawl. She heard the coo-coo clock on the wall chime each hour. She remembered that her aunt had gotten it from Germany when Joan was only ten years old. Walking through the house she was amazed at how it all looked the same as it had thirty years ago. "This is what comes of not having children," Joan thought, "You can keep things in mint condition year, after year, after year." She gently stroked the small momentous that laid out on the coffee table in Sue's den. She remembered that some of them were souvenirs from Sue's trip to 'The Holy Land'. Joan used to dream of what that trip was like.

Joan got up and went to get water from the kitchen, and took a walk outside. She found a sunny spot and sat down in the grass in the back yard. From there she could see the old barn where she had ran out each morning the weeks she had spent there as a child. There were baby kittens in the barn and she couldn't wait to see them. Her aunt had thirteen cats at one time. All outside cats, all different colors. She never turned away a stray.

Joan could see the fields surrounded by barbed wire where her uncle had kept his cows when he was alive. "Oh how he loved those cows," she whispered. She could remember they were Holsteins, and she remembered some of them having bells around their necks. She could hardly get out of the car before her Uncle Walt was taking her to the barn to get a bucket of feed to call them to the fence and let her pet them. He hadn't seemed to need the bucket though, she thought, they started coming to the fence as soon as they saw the man walking toward the pasture.

Joan remembered her Uncle Walt always smiling. She remembered hearing him down in the fields talking to the cows as he milked one or tended to their needs. She remembered how when he came home from work the first thing he did was go feed and milk the cows. It wasn't until she got older that Joan realized he had to do it that way, before it got dark. It was also after she grew into adulthood that she understood the love between Walt and Sue. It was the kind of love she now shared with James. Joan turned her face to the sky and stated, "Well Uncle Walt, your sweetheart is coming home soon, I know you're smiling now."

Joan remembered the wake that Sue had when Walt died. He laid in state in the wide hall outside the formal living room. She remembered Sue was a total wreck. Her mother had said afterwards that she would not do that if Joan's dad died first. It was years before Joan could walk by that spot and not think about that casket there with her uncle in it. "Why did Aunt Sue do that?" Joan had asked her mother this as a young child.

Her mother had explained that, "It allowed Sue to be with him every minute she could."

Only now did Joan understand.

Joan walked around to the front of the house and saw the flowers waiting to bloom along both sides of her aunt's walkway. Joan wondered who would be taking care of them now. She knew a part of her own history was dying right along with the woman inside of the house. She was happy for memories, for soon they would be all she would have left of her aunt. Joan walked back inside and found a blanket. She sat in the large rocker by her aunt's bed, curled up in the blanket, and fell fast asleep.

For two days there was little change in Sue's condition. But on the third day changes happened that Joan hadn't expected. Joan was awakened in the early morning from her bed beside Sue's hospital bed, to the sound of a rhythmic tapping. Joan knew as soon as she saw Sue that she was having a seizure.

Patricia came into the room. "What's wrong!" she almost shouted.

"Get the box of emergency medication from the refrigerator!" Joan commanded her. Her mother left and returned in short order with a small white box filled with pills, syringes, and suppositories. Joan searched quickly through the box and found the medicine she wanted. Together, the two worked until they had given three doses of seizure control medication. Then, finally, silence came from where Sue laid.

That morning about nine Joan called hospice, and Terri, Sue's assigned nurse, came out to check on them. Joan explained to Terri what was going on and Terri called Dr. Gray. By ten o'clock Sue's fever was one hundred and four degrees and the seizure activity began again. Terri and Joan worked vigorously to try to control the seizures and reduce the temperature.

"If we can get her temperature down maybe the seizures will stop," Joan told Terri.

"It will help but I'm not sure that is all it will take. Where brain injuries are involved, and the seizure isn't caused by a high fever, it usually takes more than lowering the fever to control the seizures," Terri replied without stopping her work.

After sponge bathing and giving several doses of acetaminophen to lower the fever, Joan re-checked it. "102."

"Well, that's progress, I guess," Terri replied. "Still seizing though, even with giving her all the right doses of seizure medication. I think we need more help here than we have." Terri called Dr. Gray and obtained orders for an infusion of small doses of medication through a needle placed in Sue's skin.

It took several hours for Terri to obtain all she needed and return to the house. The two nurses worked side by side for two and a half hours trying to get Sue's seizure's under control.

By the time it was over and Sue settled down Joan was ringing wet with perspiration. She left her mother to watch over Sue while she showered.

"Okay, but hurry back," Patricia's voice pleaded.

"Don't worry, I won't be long," Joan assured her. Joan returned to Sue's room after what seemed an eternity to Patricia. With two glasses of iced tea.

"I am absolutely exhausted," Joan remarked, sliding into the rocker once again. "This took so much out of me, and some of my patient's families go through this for weeks, months even," Joan stated. Sue was quiet now and in deep slumber, the way Joan had often seen people after seizure activity.

"Do you remember when you were small," Patricia spoke. "You used to beg to come here. Every year when we came here for Easter it would start. I knew you would not let up until you had your two weeks summer stay here."

"Yeah, I remember, but she made it so irresistible. I remember how spoiled she used to make me feel. We would have ice cream every night for the whole two weeks. And I always came home with new additions to my wardrobe. I remember two dresses she made me, one pink and one dark rose from the same pattern. And a beautiful brown blazer. I could never have asked for a better aunt," Joan replied and smiled.

"Remember what she used to say about Mrs. Adams' cats sitting on the fence looking at Cocoa?" Joan and Patricia laughed together. Joan continued, 'They're just mean,' she'd say, 'They're just sitting up there teasing him, because they know he can't climb up there to get them.' Truth was they were laughing at him. That little dog that she had petted so and allowed to get so fat that he couldn't chase those cats in a million years."

"You were the little girl she never had," her mother replied as she placed her arm around Joan. Tears filled their eyes.

"Do you think she feels hungry?" Patricia asked.

Joan told her, "No," and explained. "Without food or water she may have felt hungry for a couple of days but after that chemical levels in the body rise and create a euphoric state so that Sue would not feel hunger at all. And the body stops craving what it can no longer use... when people are dying."

The rest of the day was uneventful and the two caregivers

went to bed early.

At eight o'clock the next morning Joan was again summoned to Sue's bedside by the sound of seizures. She increased the medication as Terri had instructed her. She took Sue's temperature and found it to be one hundred and four again. She called her mother for help and the two worked to get the temperature down by the same methods they had used the previous day.

By ten the temperature was down to one hundred degrees but the seizure activity continued. Joan called Terri for help. Terri arrived at Sue's home at ten thirty, and called Dr. Gray. They increased the infusion once again. Terri asked for the emergency medications from the refrigerator and gave Sue two medications from the box. By eleven the seizures had slowed but were still occurring every ten minutes, regularly. Terri called Dr. Gray back, then came to talk to Joan and her mom. Joan knew it wasn't good by the way Terri sighed and cleared her throat before she began to speak.

"Look, Dr. Gray said he feels it is time we made some decisions here. He said the only thing he can think of to do now is bring her into the hospital. If we bring her in 911 he will have anesthesia ready. They will take her to the radiology department and maybe place an epidural catheter in so they can get the seizures under control." Terri explained the procedures to them as best she could.

"But," Joan stated, "If he does that they will have to hydrate her again and she will go through this all over again."

"I know Joan but that's the choice you have to make. Do you want this to continue or do you want her to be stabilized, comfortable, and returned home?" It was as simply as Terri knew how to put it to them.

Joan looked at her Aunt in the bed. And as much as she wanted to keep her home she knew this had to be uncomfortable, perhaps even painful. It certainly was painful to watch. She could feel her mother's eyes pleading with her for mercy. "Okay, we'll go in but I want her back here as soon as the seizures are under control." Joan gave in.

Joan called 911 and the ambulance arrived shortly thereafter. Terri drove Arthur and Patricia to the hospital, Joan refusing to leave Sue's side, went in the ambulance with her. Just as he promised, Dr. Gray met them in the Emergency Room along with several members of the anesthesia team. They took Sue directly into an empty operating room, the only place that was open to receive them at that time.

Joan and Patricia collapsed in the waiting room chairs. Terri told them she had to go but would check with them later. "How do you do this all the time?" Patricia asked Joan.

"I don't do this all the time, I help other people do this," Joan quietly answered.

After what seemed an eternity, Dr. Gray emerged from the double steel doors. "We have placed the epidural catheter without difficulty and the seizures have stopped. However, Sue is dying. I can offer you a private room to be with her but I don't think she would survive an ambulance drive back home."

Joan thanked him and went to call James. He agreed to go by Sue's house and get Cocoa and bring him to the hospital. James arrived at the hospital an hour and a half later. He entered the hospital quietly, trying to be inconspicuous holding the animal carrier by his side. He saw Joan before she saw him. Sitting in a chair in the hall with her legs bent up in front of her, her arms folded around them and her head down on her knees. He asked the nurse where he could find Sue. Then he took Cocoa in and placed the frightened pup in bed with Sue. Cocoa quickly snuggled Sue and settled close beside her, glad to be with his best friend.

Then James walked back to the hall where Joan was sitting. 'How small she looks,' he thought. "Hey," was all he had to say.

She knew the sound of his voice as soon as he spoke that one syllable. Joan looked up at him and the floodgate which had held back her tears for two days opened wide. "Oh, James I really messed up this time." She stood and buried her face in his shirt and her body in his embrace.

"No, you didn't, you had no idea this was going to happen. You did the best anybody could have done."

"I can't do this anymore. I can't deal with all this death and dying all the time. I had no idea it was this hard on the other side of the hospice team." Joan was crying.

James stopped her, "Now you listen to me. I'm not going to let you make that decision at this time. You are physically and emotionally exhausted. How long has it been since you ate anything?"

She didn't have an answer.

"Right now you're coming with me to get some food and calm down. You made a commitment to your aunt and to your family. You have to keep that commitment right now. But this will be over soon and you and I will discuss this in a few days... after you have had some serious sleep." And with those words James rescued her, once more. But, unlike before, he was not letting her off this time.

After they got food from the hospital cafeteria James had Joan go wash up before he took her back to be with her family in Sue's room. He also took food to the rest of the family waiting there.

Joan could see that Sue was dying when she walked in. She slowly made her way through the other family members to Sue's bedside. "I'm sorry Aunt Sue, I tried so hard to keep you at home. I hope you will forgive me. I will always love you. I will remember you as long as I live." Joan choked back tears. Then she removed the Bible from the bedside table, took off her shoes and got onto the bed. She cradled Sue's upper body in her arms and began reading.

"The Lord is my Shepherd I shall not want..." By the time Joan finished the last word of the Twenty-third Psalm Sue was still and totally motionless in her arms.

FIFTEEN

Joan returned to work the week after Sue's funeral. But she had begun to question her ability to continue dealing with death and dying on a daily basis. Her aunt's death had an effect on her that she hadn't expected. She got through her days with much difficulty.

At home she was quiet and distant. She cried a lot. James would come in from outside and catch her staring out the window. She would try to hide as she brushed away a tear. James felt unable to help her. "I've always fixed everything, the house, the cars, this family's every problem, but I am frustrated because I can't fix this," he told her.

On Monday Faye had asked Joan to meet her in the office after their team meeting. Joan wondered why Faye had called her in. She sat for about ten minutes sipping coffee and worrying what was up. Faye was always late for appointments. She was so busy. Finally she came in smiling, and shut the door behind her. Faye cleared her throat as she pulled her chair to the desk and looked across at Joan. Joan thought about how serious she looked. That made her heart pound faster and she felt a lump in her throat. "Joan," Faye began, "What's going on?"

Joan began to cry. Faye had that effect on the nurses. She knew what was going on with the nurses before she asked. Joan told her, "I've been having some trouble doing my job. I'm stopping between patients and crying. I'm distracted at the home visits and I'm afraid I might miss something."

Faye wanted her to attend the grief counseling sessions

held each Tuesday morning at hospice. She felt that Joan was stuck somewhere in her grief process over Sue's death. "I can see that you need help moving on," Faye told her.

Joan nodded in agreement with her boss's instincts.

Mike led the grief counseling sessions. Joan tried to be positive about the whole thing. She sat silently while she listened to where each member of the group was with their grief over the loss of a loved one. Some of them had been coming to the group for a year and would soon be leaving. The time limit on the group was twelve months. After that, Mike felt, if someone was still having trouble with the death of a loved one, they may need to move on to professional counseling with a psychologist.

Joan knew a few of the family members from being in their homes. She was glad to see them and it made the sessions more enjoyable to be close to them again. Some of the family members were saying good bye to the group. It was their last session and they would not be seeing many of the members in the future. A few of the members were new in their grief, like Joan. They had suffered a recent loss. They sat timidly, and cried a lot.

Mike explained the stages of grief and asked each person to write down where they thought they were in the process. Joan wrote that she was somewhere between anger and bargaining, unable to move on to acceptance. Mike then asked each person to explain why they felt they were at that stage. It was a hard exercise for Joan and the others who were new to the group.

Joan listened as each person was talking about their experience. When it was her turn she told about Sue. She learned a lot about dealing with the loss of her aunt that day. She continued to attend the group each Tuesday for three months. She was able to discuss things in the group that she was unable to discuss with anyone else.

Joan became friends with Alice, an elderly woman who had lost her husband eight months before. Alice helped Joan feel more comfortable in the group. Alice talked about the loss of her husband and how a bachelor in her neighborhood came to see her once a week. She told humorous stories about his visits and how she tolerated them. She would tell the group about how he would turn his hearing aid down when she talked to him and it would make her mad because then he couldn't hear her talk.

Alice struggled with many things that year. Her grand-children were taking advantage of her and she didn't know how to handle being courted by someone she didn't like. Sometimes Alice would fall asleep when others were talking. One day she said to Joan, "I know what your problem is."

Joan asked her, "What do you think it is?"

"You're too serious!" Alice said, and everyone laughed about how she said it.

"Well you're not the first one to tell me that, but how did you know?" Joan asked her.

"I can tell it by looking at you. The way you talk and how you hold yourself in this group." Joan just looked into the deep blue eyes of age sitting beside her and didn't say anything. She knew Alice was one hundred percent right. But what could she do about it.

Mike talked to Alice about the possibility of entering a nursing home. Alice was reluctant to do that, she wanted to stay in her home. Joan asked Alice if she had ever thought about a retirement home. She explained the concept to Alice who half way listened. Joan explained that there were several nice retirement homes around. Mike and Joan knew Alice was unable to keep her home up and her family was unable to help much. Maybe because Alice had alienated them with her dictatorial style of relating to people. Alice finally agreed to let Mike make an appointment for her to see a retirement center close to her current home.

Over the weeks that Joan spent in the group she listened to the others as they told about how the loss of their family and friends had affected them. It somehow helped her put her own grief into perspective. Before the end of each meeting Mike would have the members close their eyes and he would lead them in a relaxation exercise. That part of the session was particularly beneficial to Joan.

Joan questioned whether she wanted to remain with hospice or not. And finally she had to come to a conclusion about the questions in her mind. Joan scanned the want ads in the paper on Sunday and selected two jobs for which she could apply. She didn't feel good about it but she had to know where her heart was. She couldn't go on like this for long and she knew it. She didn't share her thoughts with Mike. She didn't feel very professional about her feelings but she still had to know.

Just before Joan left the group she found out that Alice was going to be admitted to the Heaven Sent Retirement and Senior Center. Joan was happy for Alice. She knew that they would take better care of her there than she was able to take of herself, and her family would not be able to take advantage of her there. Joan bought Alice some things for her new home and the two parted the very best of friends.

Alice enjoyed showing Joan around the grounds one Sunday afternoon when Joan visited her at the center. She showed Joan her new apartment with enthusiasm. The last thing she said to Joan was, "Life goes on."

Joan replied, "Yes it does Alice, yes it does."

SIXTEEN

Joan recognized the beautiful brunette the instant she walked into the restaurant, even though she hadn't seen her friend in over a year. Diana still looked great. She was petite, four foot eleven, with dark eyes and straight, shiny, dark, hair. She had always turned heads when she entered any room, and today was no exception. Joan watched the businessmen and construction workers watch Diana make her way across the room.

The two greeted each other excitedly. "How are you?" Joan asked first.

"Oh, I can't complain, you know... busy as always but good," Diana replied, shrugging her shoulders, "And you?"

Joan assured Diana that she was fine and the two ordered salads and tea for lunch. Joan had set up the lunch date with her friend, just after her group sessions ended. Joan had decided that she needed to spend some time away from hospice and asked for a week off.

She eased into the reason she had been driven to have some time with Diana. Perhaps she knew that her friend would not let her make a mistake. "So how are things at hospice?" Diana finally asked.

"I'm thinking about quitting," Joan told her.

Diana's eyebrows raised over the rim of her glass of tea she had lifted to her lips. "Why would you do that?" she asked.

"I'm not sure that I can do this anymore. It's harder than I thought, you know... long term. Hospice isn't just a job, it's a lifestyle. You don't just stop being a hospice nurse when your shift is over. If a co-worker needs help you go, if a family member wants to talk you stop by and see them. If someone needs something you get it one way or another. If a ramp needs to be built you have your husband do it. Not only am I a hospice nurse, my family is a hospice family. They sacrifice everyday for me to do this. It's not just a job, it's a ministry, a mission, and people who work this job well, are more like missionaries, only in their own country, not abroad. It's just so hard sometimes." Joan paused.

"I know," Diana replied. "Are James and the boys complaining?"

Joan answered simply, "No."

"Oh, I see," Diana said, trying to understand. "But hospice has changed your life remember? Remember what you told me, it's like the old Peace Corps slogan 'the hardest job you'll ever love'. Do you really want to walk out on that? You said you were thinking about it, but you're not sure right?"

Joan nodded and quickly turned away from Diana's questioning look. She had a way of looking at a person. Joan always felt that Diana could see right through to the very soul of people. Joan had once told her that she was glad not to be her child.

"I think it would be a mistake. You're too good at it." Diana told her in a very matter of fact fashion.

Joan explained to her, "Sue's death has been particularly hard for me, and now that I've put myself in the position of being a hospice family, I'm having trouble being a hospice nurse. I cry too much."

This helped Diana understand. Diana thought while she ate her salad. By the time she had finished she had decided what she should say to Joan."Remember when Allie was born?"

"Yes," Joan smiled, thinking about the memory. She was working in the newborn nursery at the time and had been present for the birth. "Yes, I remember that day very well. What a beautiful baby."

"Do you remember when the doctors told me she was in breech position and I was going to have to have a cesarean section?"

Joan nodded to acknowledge her recollection of the event.

Diana continued, "I was so upset. My first concern was for her. I wanted her to be all right but I was so disappointed because I wanted to experience everything about the birth process. All the excitement, the transition, the birth itself, even labor pains. Do you know why?"

And Joan answered, "Yes, because you're crazy."

"No, because I'm a labor room nurse. And for years I've said 'I know' when the mom's tell me how much they hurt. I had always wondered when I told them to put their chins on their chests and push the pain away, if it really worked or if it was just a bunch of words. I wanted to feel what they felt. I wanted to be able to empathize with them. I wanted to be able to say I know how they feel and really mean it. I wanted to take that baby to my breast as soon as she was breathing and comfort her and feel her bond to me immediately. When I tell the mother's about that bonding I wanted to know for sure that what I was telling them was the truth."

"So I went home and I called some experts in the labor and delivery field for help and I started getting in the knee chest position and doing exercises to help that baby turn, and she did. And I got what I wanted. I was able to do all those things, with the help of an epidural. And now I'm a better labor room nurse because I have lived it. I think hospice is like that. I think that right now you need to rest and break from it for a short time. But I think, if you will let it, that you will be a better hospice nurse now than you ever were. Because now you really know what the families are going through."

"Perhaps you're right, but I'm going for a job interview anyway. At a private pay retirement home in Charlotte. A fancy place. They need a director of home care and I think I might enjoy it." Joan surprised her.

"I think that's good. Then you can decide if you want to stay or not. That will help you decide." The two walked to the parking lot together and made arrangements to get their families together in the near future and each drove away.

Joan had made the interview appointment for late in the day. She wanted to have plenty of time to get ready. James had given her directions for the best way to get there. She almost canceled the interview a dozen times. She almost stopped her car and turned around four times while driving the thirty mile trip. She prayed for God to give her a sign. To let her know what she should do.

The home was large. It was new and updated. It was beautiful. She stood in the lobby and watched the residents going here and there to different planned activities. But all Joan could think of when she saw the residents was, "Are they really happy here? Of course they aren't," she thought, with biased opinion. Soon, a tall blond walked toward her in a fast paced style and she was whisked away to an office to talk with the administrator. After meeting the female administrator Joan didn't know whether to crawl under the desk or try to finish the interview. She looked at the lady sitting across the desk reading her resumé. Her hair was perfect, with an expensive cut. Joan estimated her suit to be at least three hundred dollars. The diamond ring which adorned her left hand was at least three carats. Her nails were perfect and polished. And Joan figured she was being sized up also.

The administrator talked in a very quick and to the point way. She seemed to have a set time to interview Joan. Joan figured about five minutes. The administrator laid all her cards on the table, and let Joan know exactly what she wanted and expected. She was looking for someone to staff an unstaffable job. She was paying relatively low wages to the staff, and offering them no benefits. The job would consist mostly of recruiting people who would be unretainable, and she knew it. She told Joan she needed someone who could tirelessly and repeatedly sell the job and recruit. Joan half way thought about it until the administrator made her last statement. "And since I am an off campus administrator you will need to be joined to me at the hip via pager or phone at all times."

Joan wanted to interrupt her with questions about where her two children came into this picture and when would she be allowed to go home, or would that be allowed at all. Joan looked at the administrator and wondered how much caffeine this person ingested in a days time. She wanted to say, "You know, I don't even know you and I'm worried about you. Are you this stressed out all the time? And is it safe for you to walk to your car alone?" But she had learned some social graces. So she sat silently.

"So with your vast experience and all your education how

do you think you would do with this challenge." The fast talking administrator was waiting for an answer. She was a little perturbed with Joan because she was taking too long to think over her answer, an obvious sign of weakness.

Joan could see she wanted a quick response, but she had to compose herself and not laugh while she found a way to tell the administrator that there was not a proverbial snow balls chance of her putting herself in this losing proposition. Joan tried to look at the administrator but all she could do was think about Winnie the Pooh trying to come up with the answer to a problem and saying to her "think, think, think."

"Well," Joan finally summoned an answer, "It seems to me that you need someone who can make a serious commitment. And before I could make such a commitment to you, I would have to seriously consider how this role would fit into the rest of my life. I would not want to waste your time by taking a job that I would not be able to commit to. So, I would have to think about all you have told me for a few days." Joan was proud of how she had said it, she thought it was a good answer, but unfortunately, or maybe not, it didn't sit well with the stressed out administrator.

She turned on Joan and said, "Well, I can see your experience is not what we need anyway. You are trapped in a dying field that the government is going to soon destroy and your job is just going to get harder. I have already interviewed thirteen people and I have three more to interview. And I don't think you are what we need here anyway."

Joan didn't say anything except, "Thank you for your time," and she extended her hand in a friendly gesture. The administrator curtly turned away.

Joan was appalled by the attitude of the administrator. She was surprised that someone in that position would talk to her in such a manner. She knew the administrator had purposefully insulted her and was smug about it. As soon as she got out of the door she laughed out loud all the way to her car. The ride home wasn't near as long or stressful as the ride down had been. She turned her eyes to heaven, "All right, I'll stay where you have me for a while longer. Thanks for the sign. You did everything except let her hit me... thank you."

James was in the garage when Joan pulled in. He came over to the Suburban and she knew he wanted to know right away if she was going to be changing jobs. But he was going to be politically correct and let her get out of the car before he asked her for an answer. "How was the drive, did you go the way I told you?" He asked.

She told him that the drive had been very pleasant and that it was only ten miles longer than the trip to her current job. She told him about the interview. "I had a date with the devil," she said, describing the administrator. "I think I'll send her some decaf to thank her for the interview."

"So, I take it you're not changing jobs after all?" James asked her.

"Well, put it this way, the Suburban needs a new clutch and an oil change, because tomorrow is another work day for me and it." Joan kissed her husband and walked inside, glad to be home.

I have skippered many a ship
My life has been full
Of seas, and inlets, and channels, and swells
Of seaspray, and sand, and salt, and palms
Of lighthouses, and piers, and ships, and buoys

I have sailed the seven continents
My travels have been broad
To Keys, and New England, and Asia, and Americas
To white beaches, and rocky shores, and reefs, and straits
To Alaska, and Maine, and Florida, and Charleston

I have been blessed beyond measure
My treasure overflows
With imported wines, and shells, and shark teeth, and sponge
With silver, and emeralds, and gold, and pearls
With conch, and starfish, and sea horses, and sand dollars

I have worked hard
My memories are great
Of sunrises, and sunsets, and blue oceans, and moon light
Of salmon, and oysters, and shrimp, and the great white
Of good friends, good mates, good food, and good times

My fears have been calmed
My soul nurtured
By meditation, and solitude, and laughter, and love
By adventure, and challenges, and thrills, and peace
By pelican, and stork, and gulls, and crane

I have lived and my life has not been without meaning
But my vessel is weak and I am so very tired
I have no more seas to sail
No more storms to conquer
No more ports to dock

The day has been long and the journey rough
My sails are tattered and my rudder is worn
I have one last mile to travel
The life flows from my hull
The wind blows gently at my back

I long for day's end
I have set sail toward the horizon
I am ready for sunset
My sails are furled with love and memories
I am complete

SEVENTEEN

"Captain my Captain," Joan said to the man sitting in the chair at the table. It was five o'clock when she got to Aaron's home.

"Come on in here, I've got a bone to pick with you," the gentleman in the wheelchair said to the nurse.

"Uh oh," she said, "I'm in trouble now," she glanced at Aaron's daughter, Lena, who was sitting at the bar smoking.

Lena had a Cheshire cat grin on her face, and raised her eyebrows as if to say, "Yes you are."

"Listen what do you mean coming in here this late in the day? You make me feel like a red headed step child," Aaron continued.

"Oh, I see. I'm sorry I should have called, but you know I have that long meeting every Monday morning," Joan tried to explain.

"Yeah, I know that, but I need to know when you aren't coming until late in case I need to go somewhere," he bargained.

"Okay, what about this, on Monday's I'll be here between four and five. On Thursdays I'll see you early, about eight or eight thirty," she offered him a compromise. "That way you can go wherever you want during the day."

"I like that plan. Then if Lena has somewhere she needs to go then we won't miss you," Aaron seemed satisfied.

"Or, if you want to go to Walmart or Walgreens..." the nurse teased him. She had learned his weakness. He smiled, caught, like a fly in her web. Joan knew what this was all about.

He had gotten his monthly check that day. And he was the 'one shoppingest' man she had ever known. Lena left the two alone.

Joan sat down and stretched her legs out in front of her, crossing them at the ankles. She asked Aaron the usual questions. How he was, did he need any medication, had his bowels moved recently. A kitten came into the room. It was small and loud and rubbing up against Joan's leg until she picked it up to pet it. "What's his name, is he new?"

"Sweetie, Lena saw him at the mall and nothing would do but she drug him home. She can't resist animals, place is like a damn zoo around here now, cats and dogs and birds and fish..." he grumbled.

Joan put the kitten down. He had began to notice the yellow parakeet in a nearby cage. Meowing he jumped on the back of a couch and looked at the bird. "That cat's going to get that bird before it's over with," she told Aaron. He turned his wheelchair around and hissed at the kitten and swatted it with the fly swat that he always kept nearby.

"I want to show you my new walker," he remembered. Joan offered to assist Aaron by going down the hall to get the walker, but he wouldn't hear of it. She watched him struggle to get the walker. He returned shortly with a multi-colored walker with a seat on it, a new style.

"Oh wow, that is nice Aaron," she enthusiastically replied.

He showed her how he was doing laps around the living area "ten times a day." He told Joan that he was exercising regularly. He was enjoying a new lease on life since he had come home from the hospital.

Joan had been seeing him for about four months when he had to be placed in the care of the Veteran's Administration Hospital because his behavior had drastically changed and Joan couldn't stabilize him at home. When he came home he looked like a different person. He was alert, energetic and cared for himself. He had resumed some of his favorite activities, cooking, shopping, and walking outside.

"Do you remember anything about before you went to the hospital? Anything you said or did?" Joan asked him.

"No, what was I like?" Aaron asked.

130

"Well," Joan told him, "You never lost your humor. You would get on to me then like you do now. You would crack jokes with me. You told me one day that I couldn't do things as good as Trisha. I told you well I'm sorry I'm not perfect like Trisha but you would just have to let me do your bath that day because she was on vacation. You asked me why she had to go on vacation and I told you to get away from you for awhile." Aaron smiled a little but Joan wandered if she had made him feel bad because so much had happened that he did not remember.

When Aaron got back to the table he was a little short of breath. Joan smiled and asked him if he had been to the new mall. "Two times!" he smiled and replied.

Joan shook her head and picked up the clipboard for the first time since she had measured his vital signs and asked him to sign her out.

"No," he told her.

"And why not?" she asked.

"Because if I do that you will go," He smiled and reached for his bi-weekly hug.

Joan laughed, "You just won't do."

Joan had discussed Aaron's case with the others. "I have to admit, it made me wonder about my mission... it has really made me question my hospice motives ," she had told Faye and the others. Rae and Beverly had told her that it was a one in a million miracle. And so as time passed on Joan had came to realize that it was.

Joan asked the new chaplain to see Aaron. "I know there are some real spiritual needs there. But I haven't been able to bridge the gap for him." She told Mary. "I'm worried because when he was so close to death before I asked him if he were afraid of dying and he nodded his head 'yes'. When I asked him if he thought he were going to heaven he said 'no'. When I asked where he was going he pointed down. I told him he is still alive and as long as he is alive there is hope. Lena is very worried about him."

Mary accepted the challenge. She spent time with Aaron. Lena and Mary both told him about the story in the Bible about the thief on the cross. Lena asked him if he believed in Jesus.

He said, "Yes."

131

"Are you sorry for your sins?" she continued.

"Yes," Aaron replied.

"What does the Bible say you have to do?" Lena was leading him.

"Believe in Jesus, and God, ask His forgiveness for sins, and invite Him into your heart?" he asked.

"Well Dad, it seems pretty cut and dry to me," Lena encouraged him.

Lena talked to Joan about it on one of her visits. "I never really knew my dad growing up. But caring for him now has given us some great quality time together, to really get to know each other. I know it bothers him that he wasn't there for me all that time. I've told him not to worry about it, that we have had this time now and that is what is really important."

"You are an absolute saint. I'm not sure I could do what you have done," Joan told her.

Aaron enjoyed his life for three more months before he began to decline. The change was very slow and he fought it the whole way. Joan kept Lena and Aaron informed of all the changes she was seeing.

"I have to know something," Joan asked him. "Do you remember before when you were so sick?"

"No." He didn't remember it at all.

"Well, before when you got very ill you wanted to go to the hospital for help. What do you want me to do this time. Do you still want to go back to the VA when you get that low again?" the nurse tried to clarify Aaron's wishes before it was too late.

"No, not this time. I'm ready to go on now. I don't think they will be able to get me this well again," he replied.

"Okay," Joan told him and made plans according to his wishes.

Lena interjected, "Our neighbor's mother died last night. You know I told you she had moved in with her son only a month ago."

"Oh yeah, I remember," Joan answered, "That was fast."

"I didn't know how to tell dad but he wanted to know what was going on over there, so I had no choice. He saw them in the yard crying. He said 'but tell them she's okay... she's an angel now, they don't have to be sad.' He was very insistent, he wanted me to take him over there so he could tell them not to worry," Lena calmly recalled the events.

"That's great!" Joan was very relieved with this change in Aaron.

The next month brought even more decline in Aaron's condition. Joan continued to prepare Lena for what was coming. Lena began to make plans for what she would do when her father died. One Monday afternoon Aaron was on the phone when Joan got to his house. "He's talking to John." Lena told her. John had been Aaron's best friend for years. Joan had met him once when he traveled from West Virginia to see Aaron. "He has cancer, he just found out today," Lena told Joan. It was difficult news for Aaron to deal with at this time, and he was crying.

Joan tapped Aaron on the shoulder, "Ask him if he has been referred to hospice by his doctor." He had not.

A few weeks later Aaron became so weak he had to be in the bed most of the time. One Monday when Joan got to his house he was watching a movie on television. Joan sat down to watch with him. They fit his visit in during commercials. "So how you doing with all this Aaron?" Joan took advantage of the fact that Lena had left to pick up her child from school.

"You know I just don't understand one thing," Aaron seemed upset.

Joan asked him, "Oh yeah, what's that?"

He gave her the news that had been eating him up inside. "You know John, my friend from home?"

"Yes, how's he doing?" she answered.

"He's out drinking at the bars celebrating. He went back to the doctor and they told him there is no sign of his cancer anywhere. He took one treatment and now he has a clean bill of health. Now he's back out drinking. I've been here trying to do everything the doctor and you tell me to do. I'm doing all I can to try to live and I'm here dying and he's out living it up," Aaron was obviously upset.

It didn't take Joan long to pick up on his message. "That seems unfair to you doesn't it?"

"Makes me very angry," Aaron confessed.

"I can understand that, and how you feel but it's in God's hands and we can't always understand why some people seem to get off scott free when others suffer. Did he have chemotherapy or radiation?"

"He had one treatment of chemotherapy," Aaron answered, still deep in his thoughts. He fell asleep before Lena got home.

"Did dad tell you about John?" Lena asked.

"Lena, there is something not right about that story. John may be in a state of denial. Or he may be protecting Aaron from more worry, but there is no way his cancer is cured after one treatment, at least not lung cancer. Aaron is pretty upset about it. But I can tell you, there's just no way," Joan was preparing to get into her car.

"You know dad always asks me what you and I talk about out here after these visits. I tell him just different stuff," Lena needed some assurance that she was doing everything right.

"He knows that we discuss him. He is probably just checking up on me to see that I'm telling him everything, not withholding information from him, you know?" Joan smiled.

Lena smiled too. Joan could see her growing weary.

Two weeks passed and Aaron became very weak. He was eating very little and his voice was barely above a whisper. He was unable to get out of bed at all any more. Joan stood by his bed side and told him, "It's time for me to get an orthderm mattress for you. It's an air mattress and you will be much more comfortable on it now that you are in bed all the time."

Aaron motioned for her to come closer to him so she could hear his request. "Why haven't you already done it?"

Joan laughed out loud, she leaned close and looked him in the eye, "You will never change."

Sweetie came into the bedroom and purred and meowed beside Aaron's bed. "Scat cat! You better get out of here," Joan waved the cat to the door.

"It's all right, he can come in here if he wants to," Aaron told Joan.

She leaned over his bed in surprise saying, "I thought you didn't like that cat."

"He grew on me," Aaron smiled.

Lena came into the room. "Did dad tell you about John?" she asked Joan.

"No, what?" Joan stopped looking at Aaron's medicines. "He died last night," Aaron said.

"Oh no, I'm very sorry to hear that Aaron," Joan offered her condolences. He wiped his eyes and turned toward the window before fading off to sleep. Lena told Joan that the news had been very hard for Aaron and she had debated not telling him, but she felt it was his right to know.

Lena went to the other room and brought back a beautifully wrapped gift and gave it to Joan. "Dad picked this out the last time he went to the new mall. He wanted you to have it."

"Thank you Aaron and Lena," Joan said as she carefully opened the gift. It was a white stuffed bear with angel wings. The tag on it read Halo.

Joan placed the bear on her vanity where she could see it daily. She wrote them a thank you card. "I will see the bear everyday and I will remember you always. I love you both." The card arrived at their home the day Aaron died. She didn't know if he ever knew that she wrote it, but she knew Lena would know and God would know, and that would have to be enough.

The day Aaron died Joan arrived at the home after his death. Lena was crying. Joan got through the usual routines and when the funeral home came to take him out she first let the family have some private time with him. Then she asked Lena if she wanted to stay there while they took him.

Lena cried and said, "I don't know."

Joan told her to come with her and she led her to another bedroom where Joan and Lena's husband held her until he was gone.

Still Joan sensed that some little something was unresolved. She asked Lena if there was something else that was wrong. Lena confessed, "I don't know if I can go through with his wishes."

"What do you mean?" Joan asked for clarification.

"The cremation, just the thought of it, I just don't know if I can do it."

"Do you want me to call the chaplain?" Joan asked.

"No, I will come to grips with it," Lena replied.

"If you don't... or if you change your mind, call us." And Joan let the subject drop.

Aaron lived a great deal in the last year of his life. Probably better than he had for a long time. Because of the loving heart of his daughter, who cared tirelessly, endlessly for his every need. And because hospice was there to help keep him living the best life he could live each and every day.

Because hospice was involved and this family was so very wonderful, Aaron and thousands more like him have been able to die peaceful deaths, free of pain and bitter harsh disease realities. Aaron knew, as do others who find themselves in the care of "hospice angels," that he mattered to the end of his life.

EIGHTEEN

Joan and James sat on the porch watching their sons play basketball on the back yard court. Chad their oldest would be going to college next year. The youngest, Brad would be getting his license soon.

"They're growing up so fast on us," Joan remarked as she took a sip of tea, and handed James his glass.

"Yes they are," James replied.

"I'm really happy I took time to be with them more at this time in their lives. We'll never have this again after next year, when Chad leaves," Joan remarked.

James nodded his head in agreement. "That was the purpose in taking the hospice job remember?"

Joan agreed, and silently thanked all her patients and hospice for showing her the real meaning of life.

HOSPICE

Hospice has it's roots in Roman times. In medieval Europe it referred to way stations where travelers could rest, women could give birth, and the ill could recover or peacefully die.

The hospice movement we know today was started in London in 1967 by Dr. Cicely Saunders. Patients were provided with better medications and families found support for the challenges they faced.

Hospice was brought to the United States in 1968 by Florence Wald, the dean of the nursing school at Yale University.

In 1998 over two thousand, eight hundred hospices cared for more than five hundred forty thousand patients. Hospice care is now covered under Hospice Medicare Benefit and Hospice Medicaid and private insurance. Studies show that Medicare saves one dollar and fifty two cents for every one dollar it spends in Hospice Medicare Benefits.

Currently hospice only cares for about twenty percent of dying people. It is the challenge of supporters of this organization to keep promoting it's missions in the most positive light possible.

There are many people who have influenced the hospice movement in the world today. I wish I could elaborate on the great efforts each of them have contributed. I am just grateful to each of my predecessors who have made this great organization what it is today.

Although we will not save lives through our campaign

we will serve our clients by making the death they must face bearable and easier to endure. We will serve each other as we struggle to give life and not death to our patient's last days on earth. We continue to enrich the lives of those patients and their families with our talents and everything we bring into their homes.

May we keep teaching and helping our communities and neighbors, and growing in our mission. May we open our arms to those who now are missing out on our services, by educating others and supporting families, nursing home administrations, and physicians. May our patients each know that they matter to the end of their life. God bless all!

Jarrett Press & Publications
Book And Product Order Form

Fax Orders: (919) 862-0991

Credit Card Orders Only: Call Toll Free: 1-888-909-7800.
Please have your MasterCard or VISA ready.

Internet Orders: *Orders@jarrettpress.com* Information: *http://www.jarrettpress.com*

Postal Orders: Jarrett Press & Publications, 2609 Discovery Drive, Suite 121, Raleigh, NC 27616
All Other Calls Please Telephone: (919) 862-0551

Please send the following books / products:

_____

_____

_____

Book orders should include ISBN: _____

☐ **Please add me to the mailing list for author book signings, public appearances, updates, and upcoming books.**

Company name:_____

Name:_____

Address:_____

City:_____ State:_____ Zip:_____-_____

Telephone: (____)_____ Fax: (____)_____

Email address: _____

Shipping: $2.00 first book $1.00 each additional.   NC addresses add 6% sales tax

Payment:
Cheque ____   VISA ____   MasterCard ____

Card number: _____

Card name:_____

Expiration date: _____

Jarrett Press & Publications
Book Publishers Since 1994

Call toll free and order now

Jarrett Press & Publications
Book And Product Order Form

Fax Orders: (919) 862-0991

Credit Card Orders Only: Call Toll Free: 1-888-909-7800.
Please have your MasterCard or VISA ready.

Internet Orders: *Orders@jarrettpress.com* Information: *http://www.jarrettpress.com*

Postal Orders: Jarrett Press & Publications, 2609 Discovery Drive, Suite 121, Raleigh, NC 27616
All Other Calls Please Telephone: (919) 862-0551

Please send the following books / products:

_____

_____

_____

Book orders should include ISBN: _____

☐　　**Please add me to the mailing list for author book signings, public appearances, updates, and upcoming books.**

Company name:_____

Name:_____

Address:_____

City:_____ State:_____ Zip:_____-_____

Telephone: (____)_____ Fax: (____)_____

Email address: _____

Shipping: $2.00 first book $1.00 each additional.　　NC addresses add 6% sales tax

Payment:
Cheque ____　　VISA ____　　MasterCard ____

Card number: _____

Card name:_____

Jarrett Press & Publications
Book Publishers Since 1994

Expiration date: _____

Call toll free and order now